Lincoln Peirce

BiG NATE

GOES FOR BROKE

HARPER
An Imprint of HarperCollins*Publishers*

For Beanie and Poppa

ISBN 978-0-06-236753-2

Typography by Sasha Illingworth
19 20 CG/LSCH 10
❖
First paperback edition, 2016

It's HANDY! It's DANDY! It's your VERY OWN

P.S. 38 DANCE MAP*

(*not drawn to scale!)

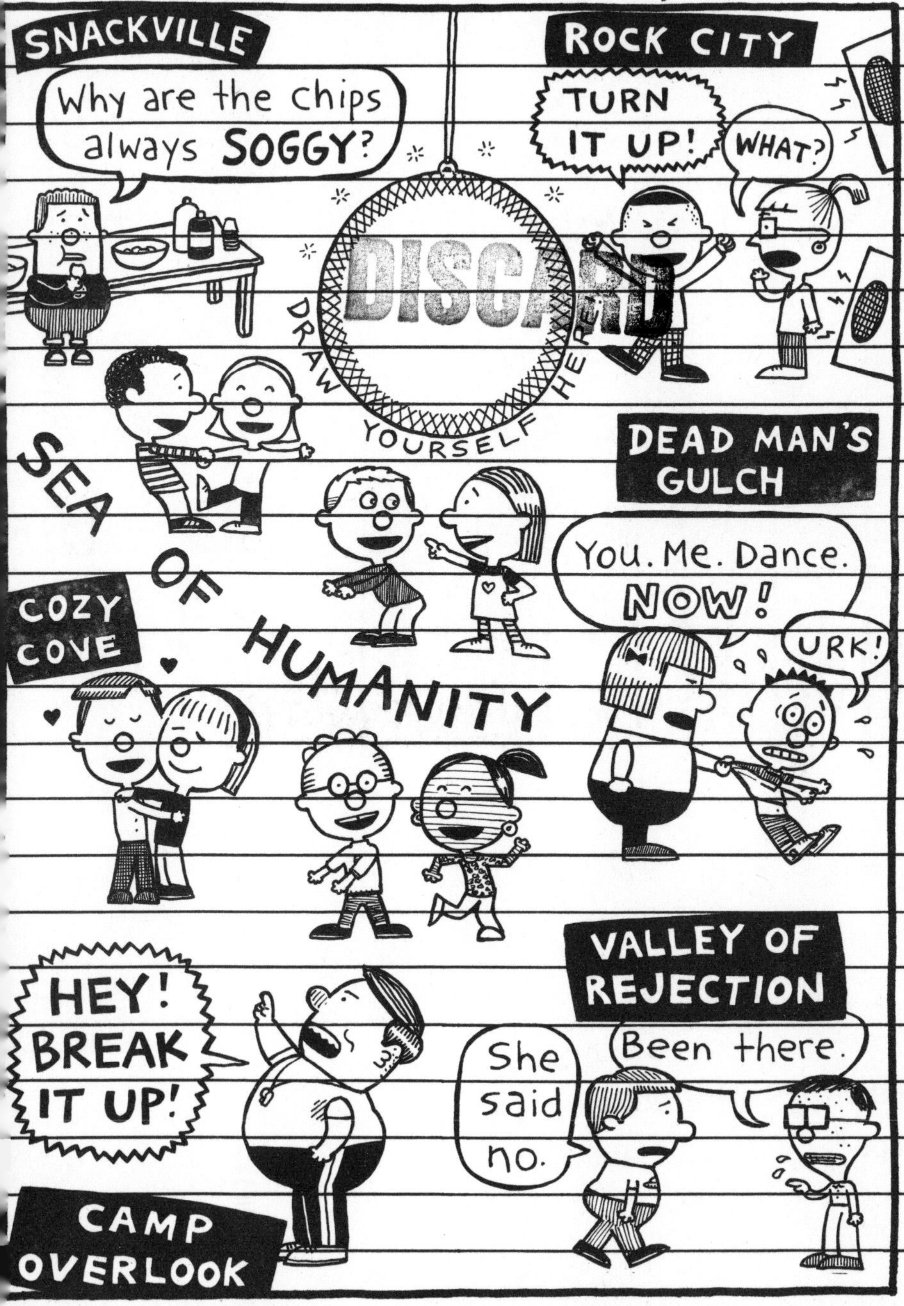
SNACKVILLE
Why are the chips always SOGGY?
ROCK CITY
TURN IT UP!
WHAT?
DRAW YOURSELF HERE
DEAD MAN'S GULCH
You. Me. Dance. NOW!
URK!
SEA OF HUMANITY
COZY COVE
VALLEY OF REJECTION
HEY! BREAK IT UP!
She said no.
Been there.
CAMP OVERLOOK

CHAPTER
1

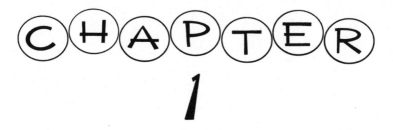

I don't want to brag or anything, but I happen to be the president of the greatest club ever invented.

Our official name is the P.S. 38 Cartooning Club, but we call ourselves the Doodlers. We meet every Wednesday after school in the art studio, and we sit around drawing comics until the custodian kicks us out. It's the best club in the whole school. By a MILE. Don't believe me? Well, then, check out this lineup.

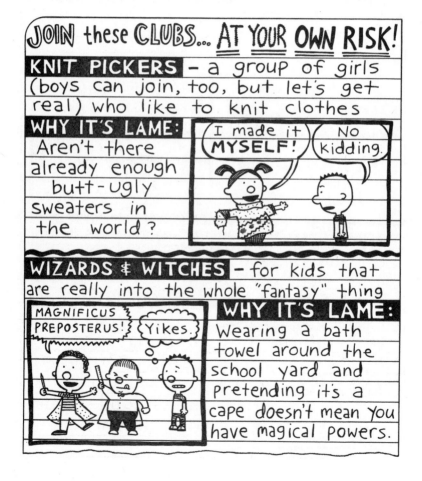

PROBLEM SOLVERS – a bunch of eggheads hanging out in the computer lab doing ridiculously hard math problems... **FOR FUN!!**

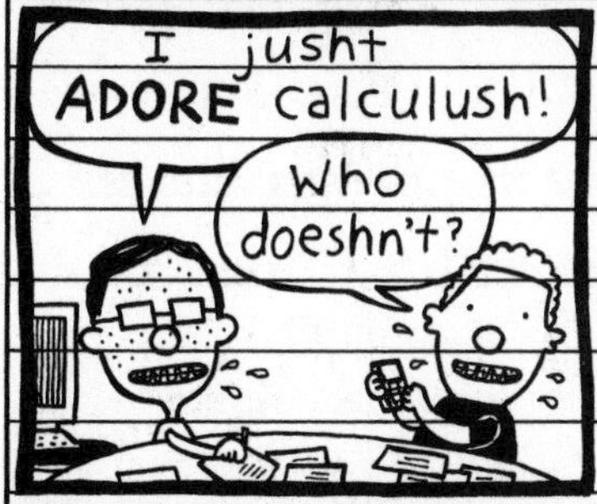

I jusht ADORE calculush!
Who doeshn't?

WHY IT'S LAME:
Isn't it obvious?

SPOTLIGHT CLUB – for kids who are convinced they're going to be huge recording stars

WHY IT'S LAME:
A. They're constantly singing in public in the hopes of being "discovered."
B. They can't sing.

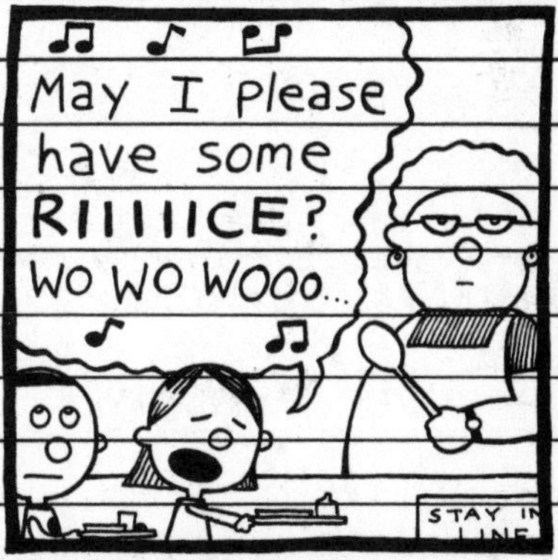

May I please have some RIIIIICE? WO WO WOOo...

SCHOOL BEAUTIFICATION SOCIETY – just what it sounds like

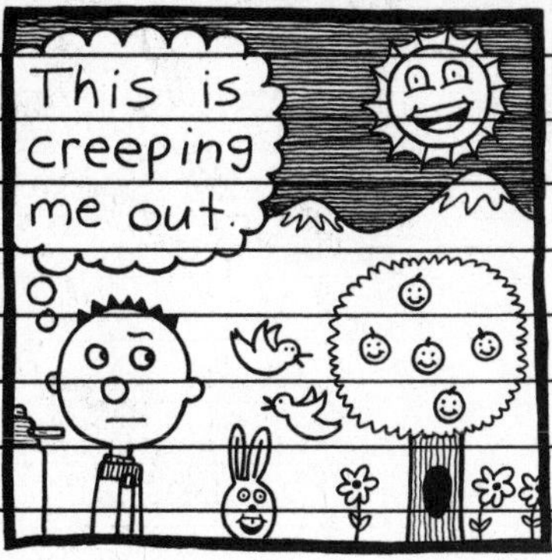

This is creeping me out.

WHY IT'S LAME:
Apparently, "beautification" means painting cheesy murals in the second-floor boys' bathroom.

See? Most of these so-called clubs look about as fun as an ingrown toenail.

But the Doodlers rock. And we only got started a few months ago. That's when it all came together . . .

...THANKS TO A GLOB OF **PEANUT BUTTER!**

DRAMATIC FLASHBACK

It was a typical social studies class.

Mrs. Godfrey was babbling about some dead guy who wasn't a good enough president to get his picture on any money . . .

Gina had already asked about nineteen completely useless questions in a row . . .

. . . and I was about five seconds away from falling into a coma.

Then Glenn Swenson walked by my desk on his way to the pencil sharpener . . .

. . . and suddenly things got a LOT more interesting!

He had food on his face. That's nothing new. Glenn usually has enough crumbs stuck on him to feed a family of four. But this was different. He had a glob of peanut butter the size of a hubcap . . .

He had no clue it was there. And neither did anybody else. It was hilarious. But I couldn't just crack up in the middle of class. Not unless I wanted She-Who-Must-Not-Be-Named to go Full Godfrey on me. So I did what I always do when something funny happens:

I drew a cartoon about it!

It was a good cartoon. Too good to keep to myself.

Teachers always ask that. What was I supposed to say . . . YES? Then even Glenn, who's dumber than a bag of hammers, would have realized I was making fun of him. And that would have been a problem, because whenever Glenn gets mad at people, he chases them down during recess and crushes them into the school yard fence until they can't breathe.

I decided I wanted to keep breathing.

Things went downhill from there. Mrs. Godfrey took my drawing and stuck it in her desk. Then she gave me a little pink slip of paper.

Hello, detention. And hello, Mrs. Czerwicki.

What could I say? She was right. But she didn't stop there. Mrs. Czerwicki didn't realize it, but the next thing out of her mouth was about to CHANGE THE COURSE OF CARTOONING HISTORY!!!

I have to admit, it was a brilliant idea—even for me. I ran and asked Principal Nichols if I could start a cartooning club . . .

Oop! It's almost 3:00. The bell's going to ring in 5 . . . 4 . . . 3 . . . 2 . . . 1 . . .

We all make a pit stop at our lockers, then head for the art studio. The art teacher, Mr. Rosa, is our faculty adviser.

Every club has an adviser. That's school policy. But most clubs have one already in place. Ms. Clarke has always run the school newspaper. And Mr. Galvin has

been the adviser for the Science Club since the last Ice Age.

That's okay if you end up liking your adviser. But what if you join some club, and the adviser's horrible? Then you're just like that glob of peanut butter on Glenn Swenson's forehead. You're stuck.

That's where the Doodlers got lucky. Since we started our club from scratch, WE got to decide who our adviser would be. I mean, can you imagine if we'd ended up with somebody like . . .

Everybody freezes. We're all thinking the same thing: What's HE doing here? Did the school switch advisers on us or something? My stomach starts churning as I picture a Doodlers meeting with Coach John in charge.

Finally Francis speaks up. "Uh . . . where's Mr. Rosa?" he asks nervously.

Coach John chuckles in sort of a scary way. Did I mention the guy's a few peas short of a casserole?

"And here I am!" comes a voice from behind us.

"Sorry I'm a bit late, everyone," he says as he takes off his jacket. Then he pats Coach John on the shoulder. "Thanks for covering for me, Coach."

Coach John grunts something in return, then waddles out of the room. Finally we can all exhale.

"Listen, gang, before we get started, there's someone I'd like you to meet," Mr. Rosa tells us as we sit down. He motions toward the door.

Colleague? What's THAT supposed to mean? This lady doesn't work at P.S. 38.

"Hi, Doodlers." She smiles as she pulls a folder from her tote bag. "I'm delighted Mr. Rosa invited me to visit with you today."

Chad raises his hand. "Are YOU a cartoonist?"

She laughs. "I'm a teacher who TRIES to be a cartoonist. But that's not why I'm here."

Whoa, WHAT? Did she say "another cartooning club"?

"We call it the C.I.C., the Cartooning & Illustration Club," she continues. "We've got about thirty boys and girls at our weekly meetings."

Uh . . . girls? I feel my face getting warm. The guys sort of steal looks at each other, but nobody says anything.

"You know," she says cheerfully, "there are plenty of girls who enjoy cartooning!" Then she spreads a whole bunch of drawings around the table.

My jaw just about hits the floor as I look down at them. Same with the rest of the guys. Even Artur's eyes are as big as pie plates. He can really draw, but some of these make his stuff look like stick figures. These drawings are PRO.

"Who—who did these?" Teddy stammers.

"Why, the C.I.C., of course," Mrs. Everett answers. "My students!"

There's a stunned silence.

"WHAT students?" Chad finally asks.

I swallow hard. I think I already know the answer. But when she says it out loud, it still hits me like a brick in the head.

Of course. Of all the schools to have a bigger and better cartooning club than the Doodlers . . .

Jefferson Middle School and P.S. 38 are archrivals. That's how WE feel about it, anyway. But the kids from Jefferson don't exactly see it like that.

And you know what stinks? They're RIGHT.

Jefferson always beats us. ALWAYS. In the whole time I've been at P.S. 38, we haven't won ANYTHING against them.

Their athletes are more athletic . . .

Their musicians are more musical . . .

Even their math geeks are geekier.

Sure, I know that winning isn't everything. How could I NOT? The teachers and coaches remind us a zillion times a day.

Have FUN? Hey, that's fine when you're six years old, playing T-ball for Little Ducklings Day Care. But after a while, that whole let's-give-everyone-a-trophy thing gets pretty tired. We're not babies anymore. We want to WIN.

"I wonder how long it's been since P.S. 38 actually beat Jefferson," Teddy says.

"What a coincidence you should mention that!" Francis chimes in. "Just for kicks, I was browsing through the school archives . . ."

"SEVEN YEARS? What'd we win at?" Teddy asks.

"Debating, I think," Francis answers.

". . . next Saturday!"

Teddy's right. I've been trying not to think about it too much—I don't want to jinx us—but our basketball team plays Jefferson next week for the first time since last year's conference championship.

What a fiasco THAT was. But this year's going to be different. We're better than we were last season, for one thing. And it's a home game for us.

A snowball slams into my head. Everything goes dark for a second, and then I land face-first in a puddle of slush. Chunks of snow are starting to slide down the back of my shirt. I jump up.

At first I can't tell who they are; they're scrunched down behind a stone wall at the top of a little hill.

But then one of them stands, and I see it: a purple jacket with gold sleeves and a big gold *J* on the chest.

We start up the hill, but it's no use. They've got a huge pile of pre-made snowballs. For every handful of snow we scoop up and throw at them, they send a dozen back at us. It's like an avalanche. There's only one thing to do:

RETREAT!

We run for half a block until we're out of range . . .
of the snowballs, that is. But we can still hear them
laughing at us . . .

...LOUD AND **CLEAR!**

"That was Nolan," Teddy says,
breathing hard.

"Who?"

"He lives near me," Teddy says matter-of-factly.
"He's kind of a jerk."

"Oh, really?" I snap, trying to shake the snow out of my pants.

I should probably explain something. Maybe you only have one middle school in your town. But in OUR town, there are FIVE of 'em. And Jefferson's close to P.S. 38. It's practically in the same neighborhood. That's why the rivalry is such a big deal: because we KNOW a lot of those kids.

"Can we talk about something besides Jefferson?" Francis says.

"Okay," he continues. "What did you guys think of what Mrs. Everett said at the Doodlers meeting?"

"I meant what she said about the club not having any girls."

I shrug. The only answer I can come up with sounds pretty lame:

"Girls can join if they WANT to," Teddy says. "It's just that none of them have asked."

"We haven't asked THEM, either," Francis says, sounding more and more like my dad. "Maybe we should."

Francis gets all exasperated. "That's the whole POINT, you pinhead!"

I know what Teddy's getting at. Yeah, there are some girls who'd probably make good Doodlers . . .

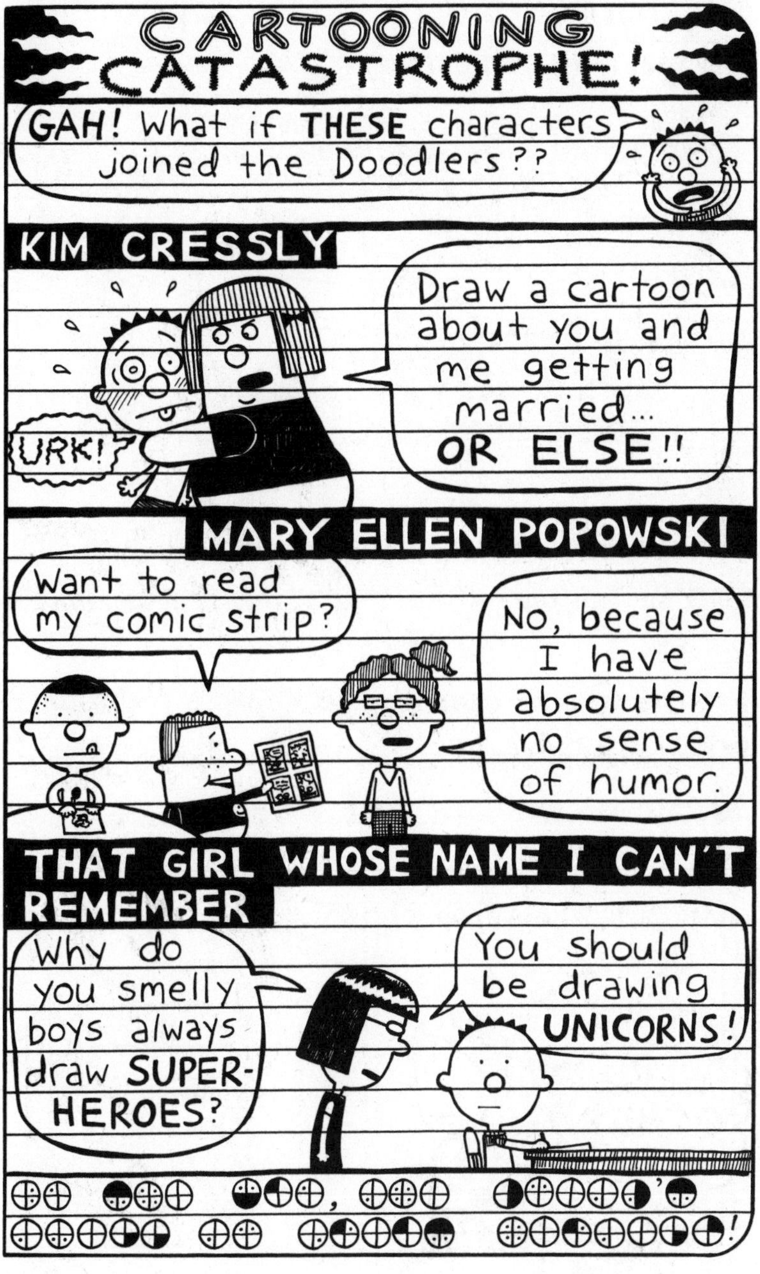
CARTOONING CATASTROPHE!
GAH! What if THESE characters joined the Doodlers??
KIM CRESSLY
Draw a cartoon about you and me getting married... OR ELSE!!
URK!
MARY ELLEN POPOWSKI
Want to read my comic strip?
No, because I have absolutely no sense of humor.
THAT GIRL WHOSE NAME I CAN'T REMEMBER
Why do you smelly boys always draw SUPER-HEROES?
You should be drawing UNICORNS!

I shiver, but not because of the snow. The thought of Gina walking into a Doodlers meeting just made my blood run cold.

"Hey, what about Dee Dee?" Francis says. "SHE'S pretty artsy!"

SHE DESIGNS ALL THE POSTERS FOR THE SCHOOL PLAYS!

"She's such a DRAMA QUEEN, though." Teddy frowns.

"Speaking of Dee Dee," I say, "that sounded sort of like her."

"It IS her," Teddy says as she comes closer. "Acting like she's onstage, as usual."

Francis shakes his head. "I don't think she's acting," he says seriously. All three of us run to meet her.

"Dee Dee! What's wrong?" Francis says.

CHAPTER 3

When we reach Chad, he's lying on his back in the middle of the sidewalk like a flipped-over turtle.

Take it easy, Dee Dee. You're not a doctor. And playing Nurse Ouchie in our second grade production of "Bunny Gets a Boo-Boo" doesn't mean you know what you're talking about.

"Where does it hurt, Chad?" Francis asks.

"My butt," Chad groans.

With a flourish, Dee Dee pulls out her cell phone.

"An emergency?" Teddy repeats. "It's a sore butt!"

"I wouldn't be so sure," Francis says as we help Chad to his feet. "I have a different diagnosis."

"How TRAGIC!" Dee Dee wails, as if we'd just told Chad he has two weeks to live.

See why Teddy called her a drama queen? She can take any situation and turn it into a major theatrical production. Starring herself.

We ignore her. "Can you walk?" I ask Chad.

He takes a couple steps, then winces. "I CAN," he says miserably. "But it doesn't feel very good."

So Dee Dee calls Chad's mom, and we wait with him until she shows up.

"Alas," says Dee Dee as they drive off. "Poor Chad."

Poor Chad is right. The next day in school, he's sitting on a donut.

A MEDICAL donut, I mean. It's a giant inflatable ring, almost like a life preserver. When he walks from class to class, it looks like he's carrying a toilet seat.

So Francis was right. It WAS his tailbone.

I feel bad for Chad. Not just because he's hurt, but because . . . well, having a bruised tailbone is sort of embarrassing, don't you think? I mean, when you're talking about different kinds of injuries . . .

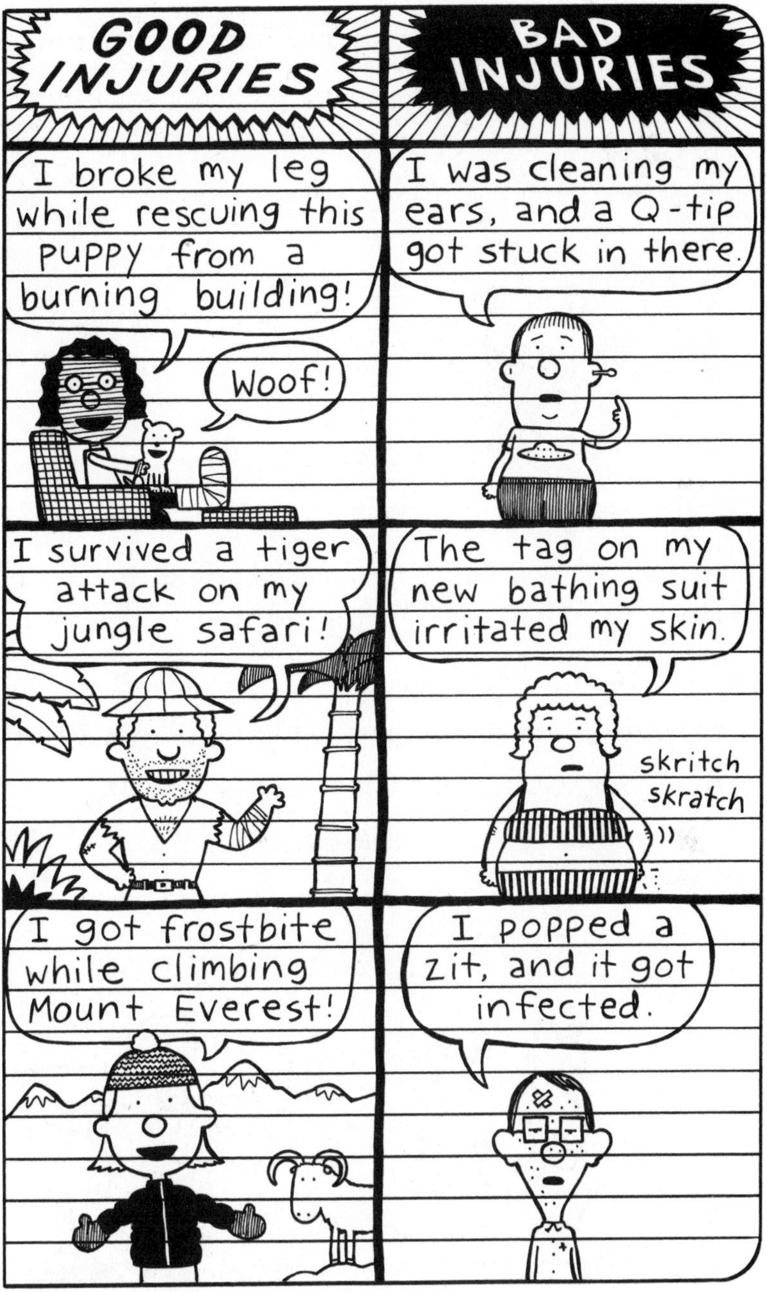
GOOD INJURIES
BAD INJURIES
I broke my leg while rescuing this puppy from a burning building!
Woof!
I was cleaning my ears, and a Q-tip got stuck in there.
I survived a tiger attack on my jungle safari!
The tag on my new bathing suit irritated my skin.
skritch
skratch
I got frostbite while climbing Mount Everest!
I popped a zit, and it got infected.

I've been lucky. I've never had one of those really embarrassing injuries.

"Good gravy!" Mr. Rosa yelps in surprise. "Nate, are you all right?"

"Yeah. I'm okay," I say as I get off the floor.

"Well, since you're all here," Mr. Rosa continues, "I'd like to mention that Mrs. Everett made a good point yesterday . . ."

Not THIS again. Why do we have to change the club? Why mess with perfection?

"Boys aren't the ONLY ones who wind up in detention for drawing comics." Mr. Rosa chuckles. "Girls can be pretty cartoony, too!"

We watch as he disappears down the hallway. "Recruiting," I grumble. "Whoop-de-stinkin'-do."

"Who are we supposed to recruit?" Teddy wonders.

Uh, right WHERE? All I see is a poster for the dance tomorrow night.

"DEE DEE drew that!" Francis explains.

I examine the poster. Okay, three cheers for Dee Dee. She can draw a half-decent seagull. But why does that mean she gets to join the Doodlers? I don't want our meetings

turning into the Amazing Dee Dee Show.

"Aren't there any other girls we can recruit?" I ask hopefully.

Teddy jumps in. "What about Jenny?"

I cringe. Jenny would be an AWESOME Doodler. That's obvious. But there's one huge problem:

And—don't ask me why— Jenny and Artur are still an item. So if she joined the club, Wednesday afternoons would probably turn into . . .

Ugh. I'm supposed to draw comics while those two count each other's freckles? I'd rather eat egg salad. Hey, I'd rather BATHE in egg salad.

"I already talked to Jenny," I lie. "She can't do it."

"Then it's decided!" Francis declares with a clap of his hands. "Dee Dee it is!"

Teddy grimaces. "Who's going to ask her?"

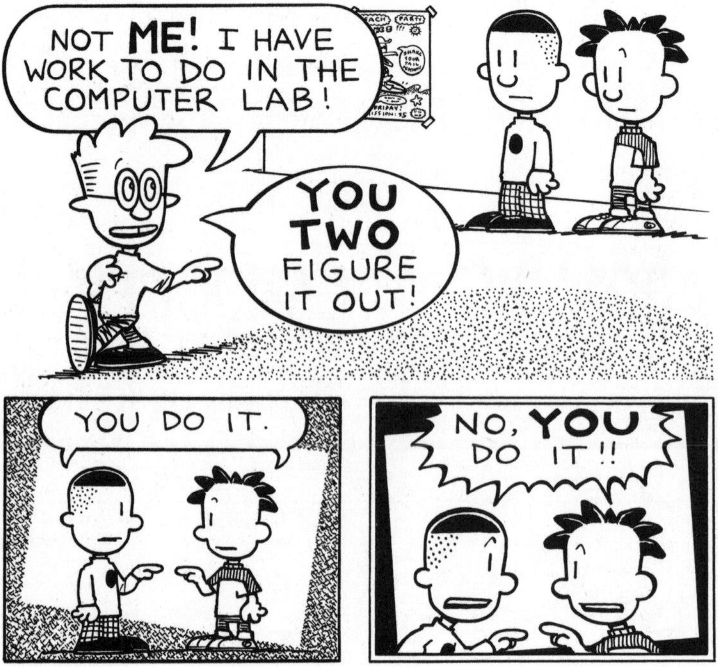
NOT ME! I HAVE WORK TO DO IN THE COMPUTER LAB!
YOU TWO FIGURE IT OUT!
YOU DO IT.
NO, YOU DO IT!!

"We'll shoot for it," Teddy says. "Odds or evens?"

"Evens," I say automatically. I ALWAYS pick evens.

ONCE...
    TWICE...
        THREE TIMES...

...SHOOT!

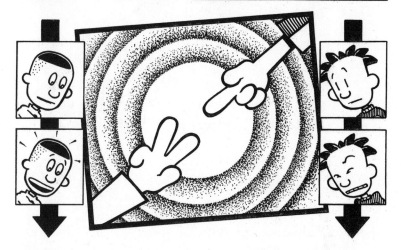

ODDS! I WIN!

CONGRATULATIONS, NATE! THE JOB'S ALL **YOURS!**

Rats. I KNEW I should have picked odds.

I walk into the cafetorium, racking my brain for a way to weasel out of this. Then I remember the last thing Mr. Rosa told us:

And talk about timing. Guess who's sitting at the very first table? Dee Dee and her flock of BFFs from the Drama Club.

She doesn't hear me. Why am I not surprised?

"DEE DEE!" I yell a few dozen times. Finally she turns around.

"What is it, Nate?" Dee Dee says.

"Hm? Uh . . . well, it's . . ." I stammer. "I . . . um . . . wanted to ask you something."

"Okay, go ahead!"

A half-eaten sandwich flies past us, nearly clocking me in the head. For a second, I lose my train of thought.

"I . . . uh . . . I forgot what I was saying," I tell her, a little flustered.

"It's okay," Dee Dee chirps. "I know what you were about to ask, and SURE! . . ."

CHAPTER 4

Okay, let's get something straight: I'd ask MRS. GODFREY to the dance before I'd ask Dee Dee. But I guess that doesn't matter now.

What matters is, she THOUGHT I was asking her. Before I could explain, she'd already turned lunch-time into show-and-tell.

Dee Dee has a voice that could blow a hole in a battleship, so right then and there the whole cafetorium knew: She and I were going to the dance together.

That's how I ended up here: half a block from her

house at 7:10 on Friday night.

For a second, I think about going home. But that would never work. The Parent Patrol would see to that.

Besides, I don't want to miss the dance. They're cheesy, but I LIKE school dances. And I actually know what I'm doing out there—unlike SOME people. Check out these so-called moves:

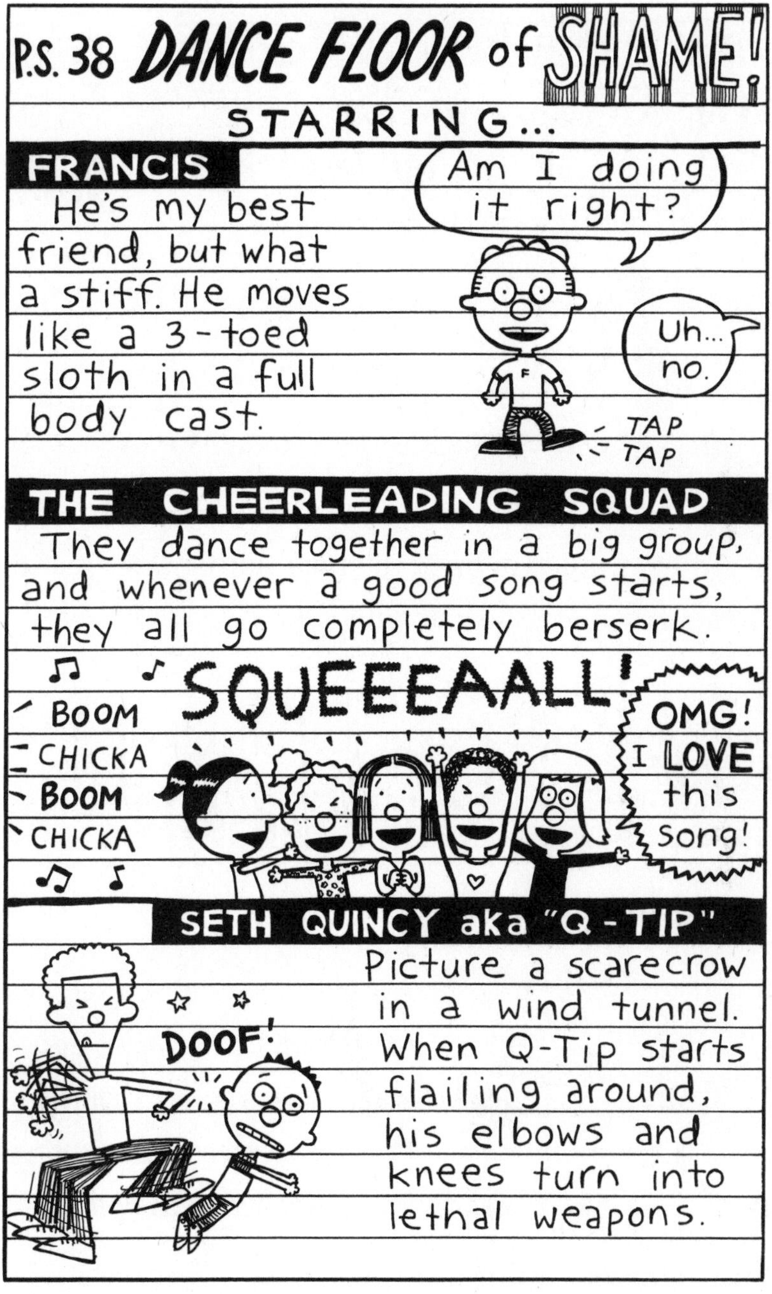
P.S. 38 DANCE FLOOR of SHAME!
STARRING...
FRANCIS
He's my best friend, but what a stiff. He moves like a 3-toed sloth in a full body cast.
Am I doing it right?
Uh... no.
TAP TAP
THE CHEERLEADING SQUAD
They dance together in a big group, and whenever a good song starts, they all go completely berserk.
BOOM CHICKA BOOM CHICKA
SQUEEEAALL!
OMG! I LOVE this song!
SETH QUINCY aka "Q-TIP"
Picture a scarecrow in a wind tunnel. When Q-Tip starts flailing around, his elbows and knees turn into lethal weapons.
DOOF!

Anyway, it looks like I'm stuck taking Dee Dee to the dance. But how do I do it . . .

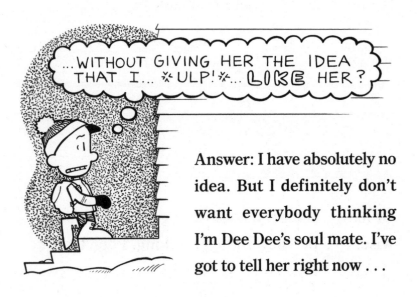

Answer: I have absolutely no idea. But I definitely don't want everybody thinking I'm Dee Dee's soul mate. I've got to tell her right now . . .

Yikes. Where did Dee Dee shampoo her hair—
in the produce section at Grocery Town? I'm so
surprised by the pyramid of fruit on her head that
I forget about my "just friends" speech. I guess I'll
tell her while we walk to the dance.

Or maybe not. I try, but I can't get a word in edge-
wise. Dee Dee never stops yakking. I don't get it:
When does she come up for air?

By the time we reach the school, I've heard enough of the World According to Dee Dee to last awhile. Like forever. We step into the lobby and . . .

Ugh. It's Randy Betancourt, P.S. 38's resident scuzzball. He's just like Chad's tailbone: a total pain in the butt.

He snickers and shoots us one of his typical Randy smirks. Briefly, I consider hitting him in his big fat nose with a piece of fruit. After all, Dee Dee's got a head full of ammo. Then . . .

The smirk slides off Randy's face in half a heartbeat. He looks totally stunned. Hey, I'm a little stunned myself. Did that just really HAPPEN?

She shrugs. "He deserved it," she says as we hang up our coats. "If two friends want to go to a dance together . . ."

I could remind Dee Dee that SHE can make a big deal out of sharpening a pencil, but I decide not to. I'm too busy breathing a huge sigh of relief. Did you hear what she just called us?

So she DOESN'T like me! Not in "THAT" sort of way. I can relax. Dee Dee's not going to turn all sappy and start calling me stupid pet names like Lamb Chop, Dumpling Face, Puffy Bunny, Snuggle Bug . . .

. . . HONEYBEE, SUGAR BOOGER, PASSION PANDA . . .

NATE! . . . HELLOooo? NATE!

I'M GOING TO CHANGE INTO MY BEACH CLOTHES.

Good idea. I grab my backpack and slip into the bathroom. I'm still feeling pretty pumped. Knowing Dee Dee isn't

BOYS

all gung ho to make me her love monkey has flipped this whole evening completely around.

He disappears, and all my clothes go with him. I look down at what I'm wearing, and a sick feeling settles in my gut. Tighty-whities and a pair of tube socks won't cut it as "beach attire."

I peek out, hoping I'll spot a friendly face. And hoping nobody spots ME. It would be just my luck to run into a reporter from the school newspaper right about now.

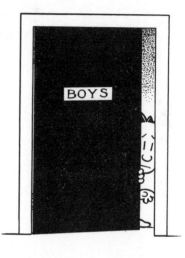

The lobby's empty. Everybody's gone into the gym. Unless I want to stroll in there looking like an escapee from a nudist colony, I'm stuck.

She stops, then inches slowly toward me. "Nate?" she asks. "What are you doing?"

I hesitate. This is pretty embarrassing. But what do I have to lose? We're FRIENDS, right? Dee Dee said so herself. And I need help.

She scowls. "He's an even bigger moron than I THOUGHT he was," she grumbles. Then her face brightens.

Wait right here? That's hilarious. Where does she think I'd go?

This must be some Drama Queen Rule: Always be ready for a costume change. I don't know what's in that bag, but I'm not picky. It's got to be better than what I'M wearing.

"You look fabulous!" Dee Dee beams.

"FABULOUS?" I shout in disbelief. "I'm wearing a DRESS!"

"It's a grass skirt, genius," she says matter-of-factly as she drags me toward the gym.

Great. Hawaii is five thousand miles away, and I look like an idiot. But why sweat the details?

Into the gym we go, with me praying that everyone's too busy dancing to notice me. But then . . .

A bunch of kids gather around. I brace myself.

Wait, what's going on here? No finger pointing? No insults? What's WRONG with these people?

"That's AMAZING, Nate!" someone says. "You look just LIKE them!"

I'm about to ask who "them" is . . . and then I look up at the stage.

I'm dressed exactly like the band. Or they're dressed exactly like me.

"You must KNOW those guys, right?" one kid says.

"How'd you pull it off, Nate?" asks another.

"It . . . well . . . uh . . ." I stammer. I can't think of a single word to say. But Dee Dee can.

And that's that. I get a few more compliments, and then everybody starts dancing again, leaving me and Dee Dee standing by the snack table.

Hmmm. NOW what? I should probably say something to her, like:

That's not what comes out, though. Instead, it's:

"From the Drama Club," she says. Then she strikes a pose and gives a sigh so huge, it practically blows my shirt off. "I just love the Drama Club."

Yes, Dee Dee, we know. Without the Drama Club, life would have no meaning.

Suddenly I remember what I was doing when this whole thing started: RECRUITING!

I tell her about the club and what an awesome adviser Mr. Rosa is. I talk about the fun drawing games we play at meetings, like Add-On, Connect-the-Freckles, and Going, Going, Godfrey.

"AND," I add, "if you join, you'll be the first girl Doodler EVER."

"I'm in," she announces immediately.

"Excellent!" I say, and I mean it, too. Sort of.

"Let's boogie!" Dee Dee shouts, and she and I hit the dance floor.

Whew. Except for the fact that my clothes are probably stuffed in a garbage can somewhere, this all turned out pretty well! I still

think Dee Dee needs to hit the off button on the drama-tron, but she kept this dance from becoming a total disaster. She's okay.

"Do you feel something wet?" she asks suddenly.

Huh? WET? That's weird. Maybe one of those tangerines on her head just sprang a leak.

CHAPTER 5

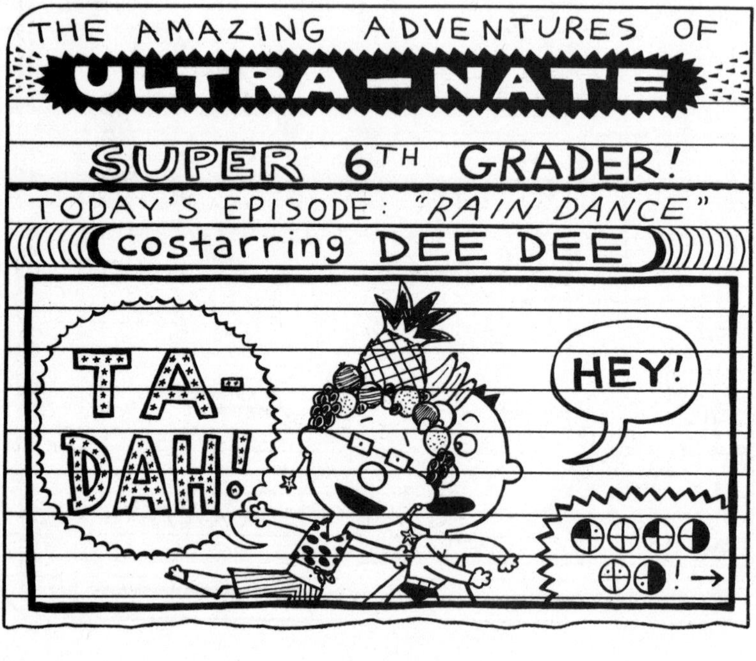
THE AMAZING ADVENTURES OF
ULTRA-NATE
SUPER 6TH GRADER!
TODAY'S EPISODE: "RAIN DANCE"
costarring DEE DEE
TA-DAH!
HEY!

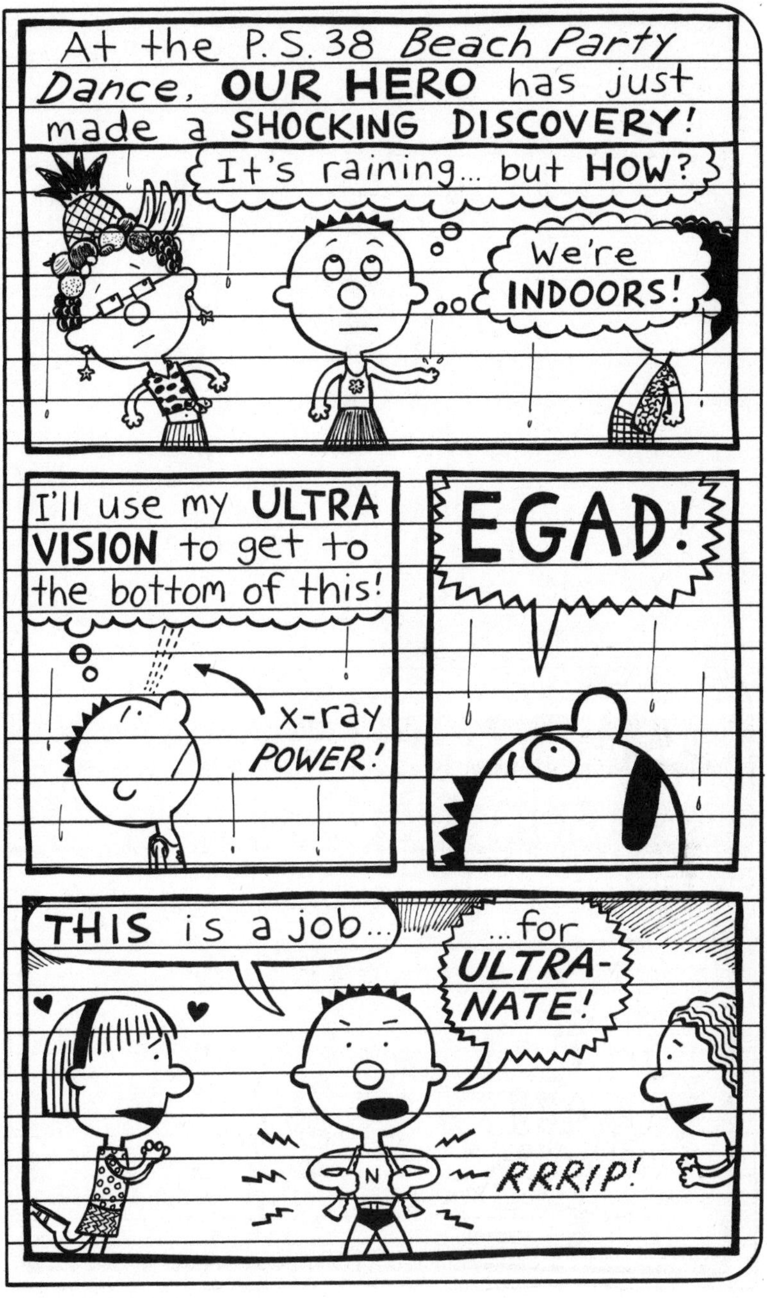
At the P.S. 38 *Beach Party Dance*, **OUR HERO** has just made a **SHOCKING DISCOVERY!**
It's raining... but **HOW?**
We're **INDOORS!**
I'll use my **ULTRA VISION** to get to the bottom of this!
x-ray *POWER!*
EGAD!
THIS is a job...
...for *ULTRA-NATE!*
RRRIP!

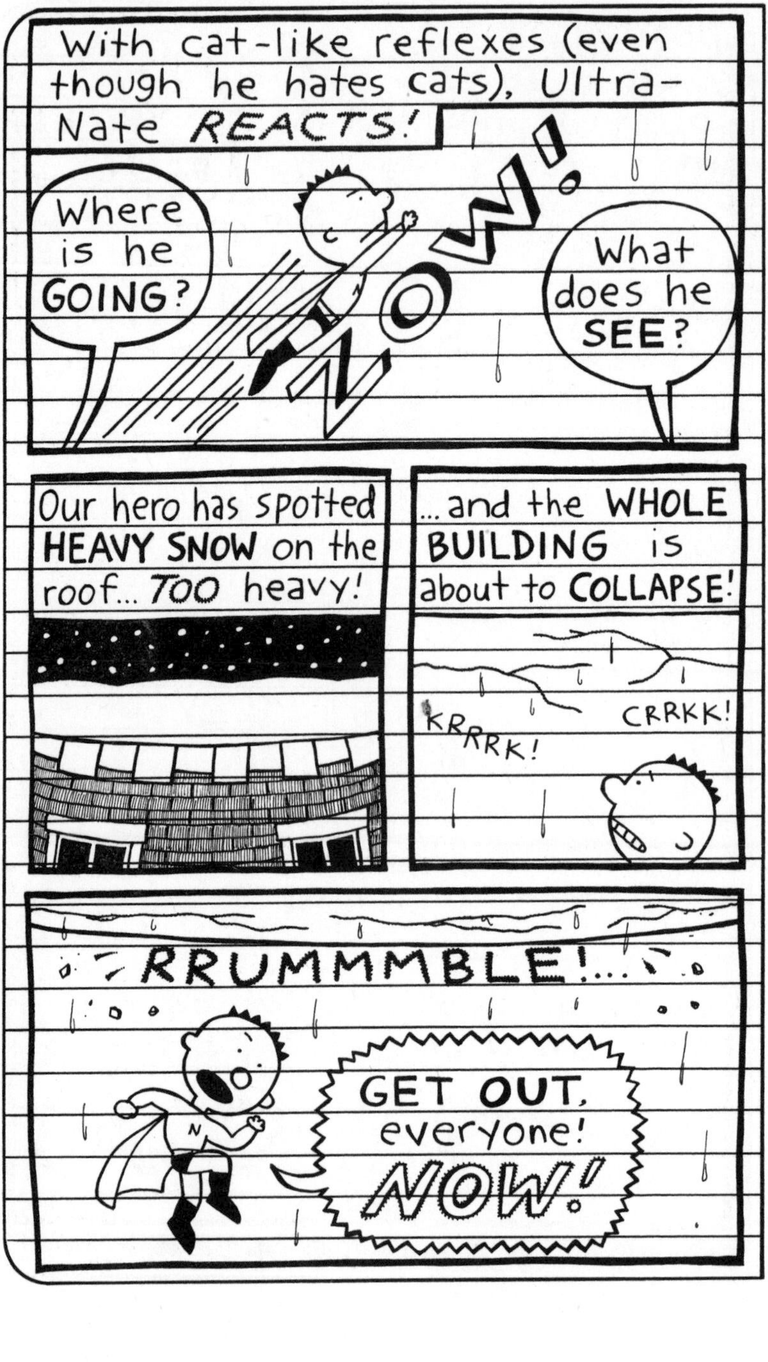
With cat-like reflexes (even though he hates cats), Ultra-Nate REACTS!
Where is he GOING?
ZOOM!
What does he SEE?
Our hero has spotted HEAVY SNOW on the roof... TOO heavy!
...and the WHOLE BUILDING is about to COLLAPSE!
KRRRRK!
CRRKK!
RRUMMMBLE!...
GET OUT, everyone! NOW!

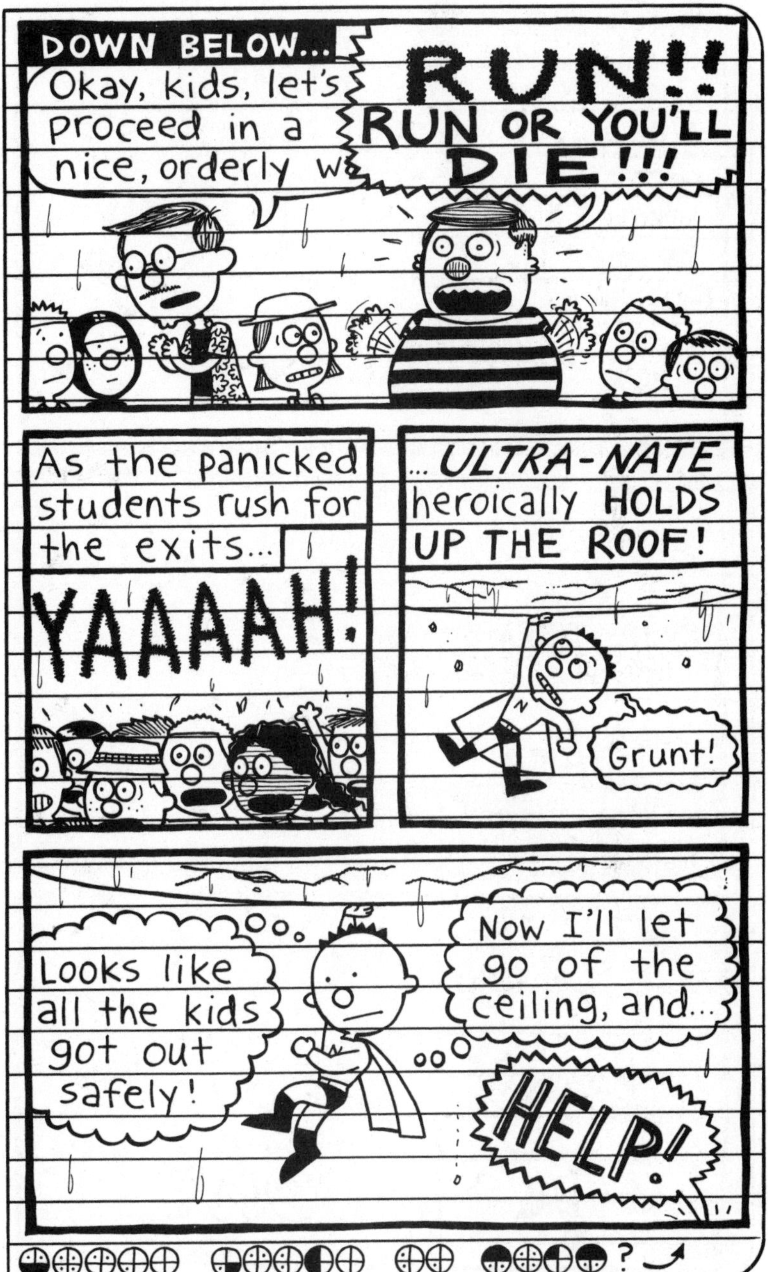
DOWN BELOW...
Okay, kids, let's proceed in a nice, orderly w
RUN!! RUN OR YOU'LL DIE!!!
As the panicked students rush for the exits...
YAAAAH!
...ULTRA-NATE heroically HOLDS UP THE ROOF!
Grunt!
Looks like all the kids got out safely!
Now I'll let go of the ceiling, and...
HELP!

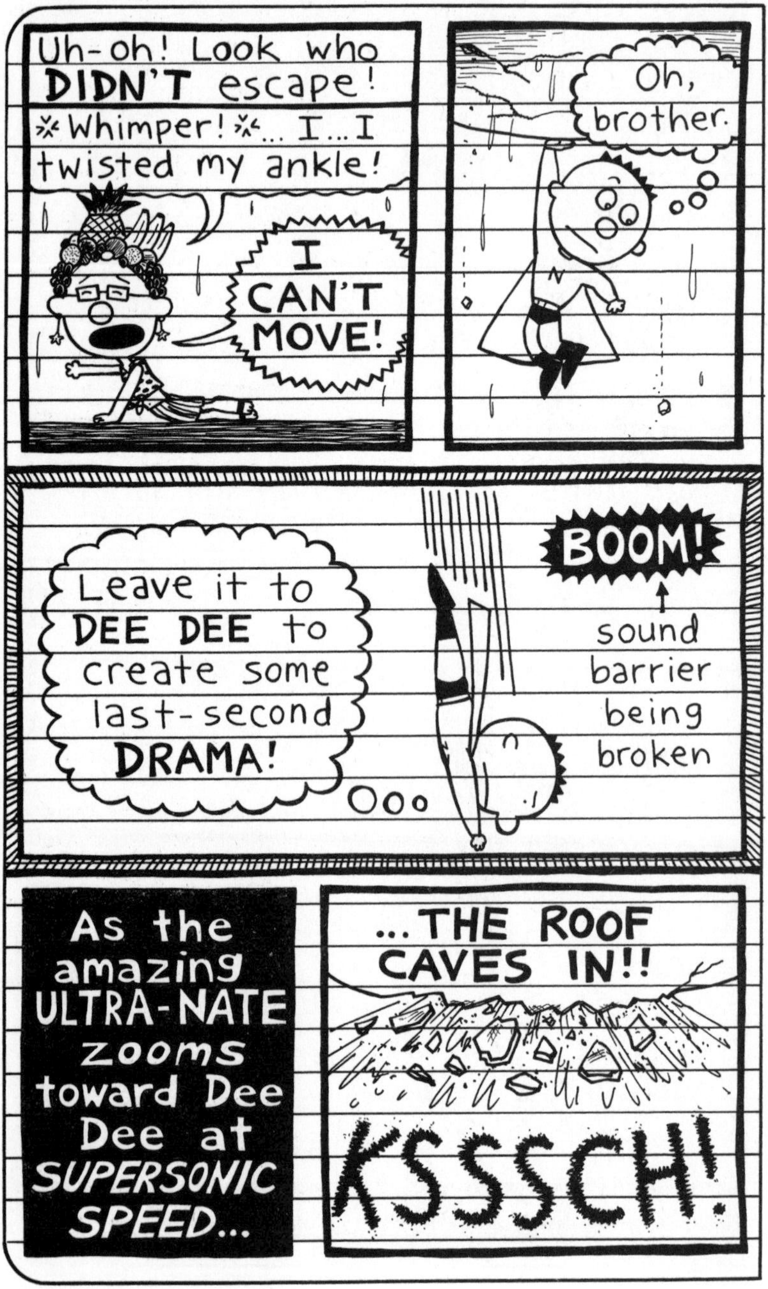

Uh-oh! Look who DIDN'T escape!
Whimper! ... I ... I twisted my ankle!
I CAN'T MOVE!
Oh, brother.
Leave it to DEE DEE to create some last-second DRAMA!
BOOM!
sound barrier being broken
As the amazing ULTRA-NATE zooms toward Dee Dee at SUPERSONIC SPEED...
... THE ROOF CAVES IN!!
KSSSCH!

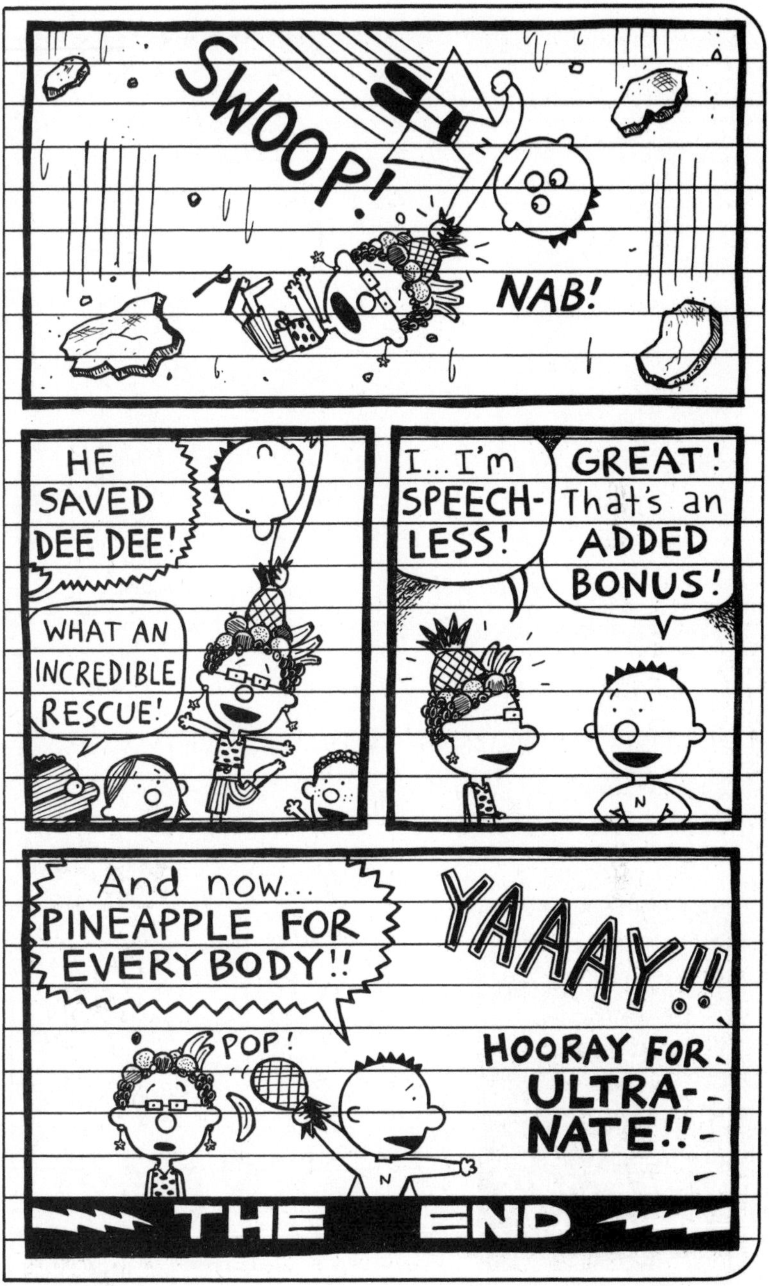
SWOOP!
NAB!
HE SAVED DEE DEE!
WHAT AN INCREDIBLE RESCUE!
I... I'm SPEECH-LESS!
GREAT! That's an ADDED BONUS!
And now... PINEAPPLE FOR EVERYBODY!!
YAAAY!!
POP!
HOORAY FOR ULTRA-NATE!!
THE END

Okay, it might not have happened EXACTLY like that. I was using a little something we cartoonists call artistic license.

But it DID start raining inside the gym. And I DID come to Dee Dee's rescue . . . sort of. Here's the real story:

The chaperones didn't even NOTICE the rain at first. They were too busy stuffing their faces at the snack table. But then the fire alarm went off. THAT made them step away from the bean dip.

But there wasn't a fire. And the rain wasn't coming from a leaky roof, either. After they'd hustled us out of the gym and into the lobby, Principal Nichols explained what was going on.

Dee Dee looked crushed. "Well, THAT isn't very dramatic," she grumbled.

"I'm afraid we'll have to end the dance a little early," Principal Nichols went on.

THEN things got crazy. We were all looking for our stuff in a giant mosh pit, it was still raining, the fire alarm was still ringing, and Coach John was marching around like a deranged drill sergeant.

Once I stepped outside, it was like walking into a giant snow globe. Don't get me wrong— I love snow. But ever wear a grass skirt in a blizzard? My butt felt like a frozen Popsicle.

Mmm, marshmallows! My favorite food group. I started to follow the guys, but then . . .

"Uh . . . maybe they'll show up in the lost and found on Monday," I told her. Translation: Life happens, Dee Dee. Deal with it.

"But what about NOW?" she wailed. "I can't walk home in the snow wearing SANDALS!"

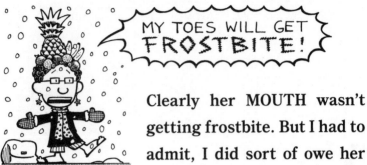

Clearly her MOUTH wasn't getting frostbite. But I had to admit, I did sort of owe her one. If it wasn't for Dee Dee . . .

Talk about a lousy end to a lousy night. Not only did I carry Dee Dee home on my back, I had to listen to her reenact scenes from her favorite horse movies.

Note to self: NEVER, not even by accident, invite a girl to a dance again.

I see a blinking light flash from Francis's window. That's our secret signal! I grab my binoculars and peer through the snow across the yard.

Tomorrow can't get here fast enough!

At exactly 10:00 the next morning, Francis and I are standing at the base of Cluffy's cliff. It's not really  a cliff, I guess. But it's the steepest hill in town. It's perfect for sledding.

"I wonder where Teddy is," I say.

Francis's eyes widen as he looks behind me. "Wow!" he shouts. "TEDDY!"

A **SUPA-SNO TUBE!** DUDE! WHERE'D YOU **GET** THAT?

"Bought it myself!" Teddy answers proudly. "I saved the money I made shoveling driveways!"

Now I'm REALLY stoked about taking on Cluffy's cliff. We hike up to the top and, after going on a couple runs himself, Teddy lets Francis and me have a turn. It's amazing.

"That's WAY faster than a plain old snow saucer!" I whoop after my first ride.

"I wonder what the speed record is for snow tubes," Francis says.

"Go look it UP, geek," says a gruff voice.

MEANWHILE, **WE'LL** BORROW YOUR NEW **TOY!**

It's Nolan, the kid who ambushed us the other day. And it looks like he's got half the Jefferson wrestling team with him.

"We're using it right now," Teddy tells him.

"Aw, come ON!" Nolan says in a fake, you-just-hurt-my-feelings voice.

He snatches it right out of Teddy's hands. Then he and his crew pile on top of it.

"Hey, get OFF!" Teddy shouts. "It can only hold two people!"

They push off down the hill. But they don't get far. They catch air going over the first bump, and . . .

DISASTER!!

By the time the three of us reach the tube, it's flat as a pancake, and Nolan and his gang are walking away.

"BAD NEWS, chump!" he calls.

It's a helpless feeling. What are we going to do, try and FIGHT them? Those guys are huge. They'd give us the worst face wash we ever had.

Teddy's about to cry, and I don't blame him. "I only got to ride it twice," he says miserably.

"Let's take it back to my house," I say. "We can try to patch it." But we can all see it's beyond patching.

We trudge along in silence until . . .

A bunch of vans and trucks are lined up in front of P.S. 38 like it's afternoon car pool time. What's with all the action on a Saturday?

"That's Dee Dee's dad!" Francis says, pointing to a beefy guy on the sidewalk.

"Eventually," he says. "But first we've got to clean up. It's a MESS in there."

You want to clean up the mold? Easy. Shut down the hot lunch program.

Francis looks puzzled. "But how can we have school with all THAT going on?" he asks.

Dee Dee's dad shrugs. "You CAN'T," he says.

CHAPTER 6

Welcome to the happiest day of my life.

"Yes, I know," Dad says as we all peel off our snow gear. "I just read an email from your principal."

IT EXPLAINS THE SPRINKLER MALFUNCTION, THE CLEANUP EFFORT, THE TIMETABLE FOR REOPENING...

"Does it ALSO explain my master plan for Monday morning?" I ask. "I'm going to wake up early, go stand in the driveway . . ."

...AND **WAVE** AT THE **JEFFERSON BUS** AS IT ROLLS BY!

Have fun at **SCHOOL**, kids! Study **HARD**!

Nyuk! Nyuk!

still wearing jammies →

JEFFERSON MIDDLE SCH

Dad shoots me an odd little smile. "Speaking of Jefferson . . ." he begins.

I groan. "Ugh. Can we not talk about Jefferson, Dad? That whole school is Jerk Central."

He raises an eyebrow. "Really?" he asks. Then he shrugs. "All right, I won't say another word."

Huh? Why, so we can read Principal Nichols's thrilling description of mildew in the teachers' lounge? No, thanks. We've got better things to do.

Francis looks at Dad's laptop. "You can forget about that vacation," he says. "Listen to this:"

> During the restoration of P.S. 38, no class time will be missed. Our top priority is to make certain that teaching and learning continue without interruption.

"WHAT??" Teddy and I cry in unison.

"In other words, we still have to go to school," Francis says.

"Where, in an IGLOO?" Teddy asks.

Francis keeps reading. "'For the next two weeks, classes will be held on the campus of our sister institution . . .'"

It can't be true. THIS IS AN OUTRAGE!!!

But then Francis and Teddy call home, and guess what? Their parents got the exact same email. What a punch in the gut.

I feel flatter than Teddy's snow tube. Going to another school for two weeks is lousy enough . . . but JEFFERSON?? They already think we're pathetic. This pretty much proves it.

"I'm takin' off," Teddy mutters.

I know what they mean. The day went bad faster than Dad's tuna casserole. I watch them leave, trudge upstairs to my room, and flop onto my bed.

I've been here before. (And no, I don't mean in bed. Duh.) I mean, I've been in a SITUATION like this, where something that SEEMED great turned into a giant turd fest. Here's what happened:

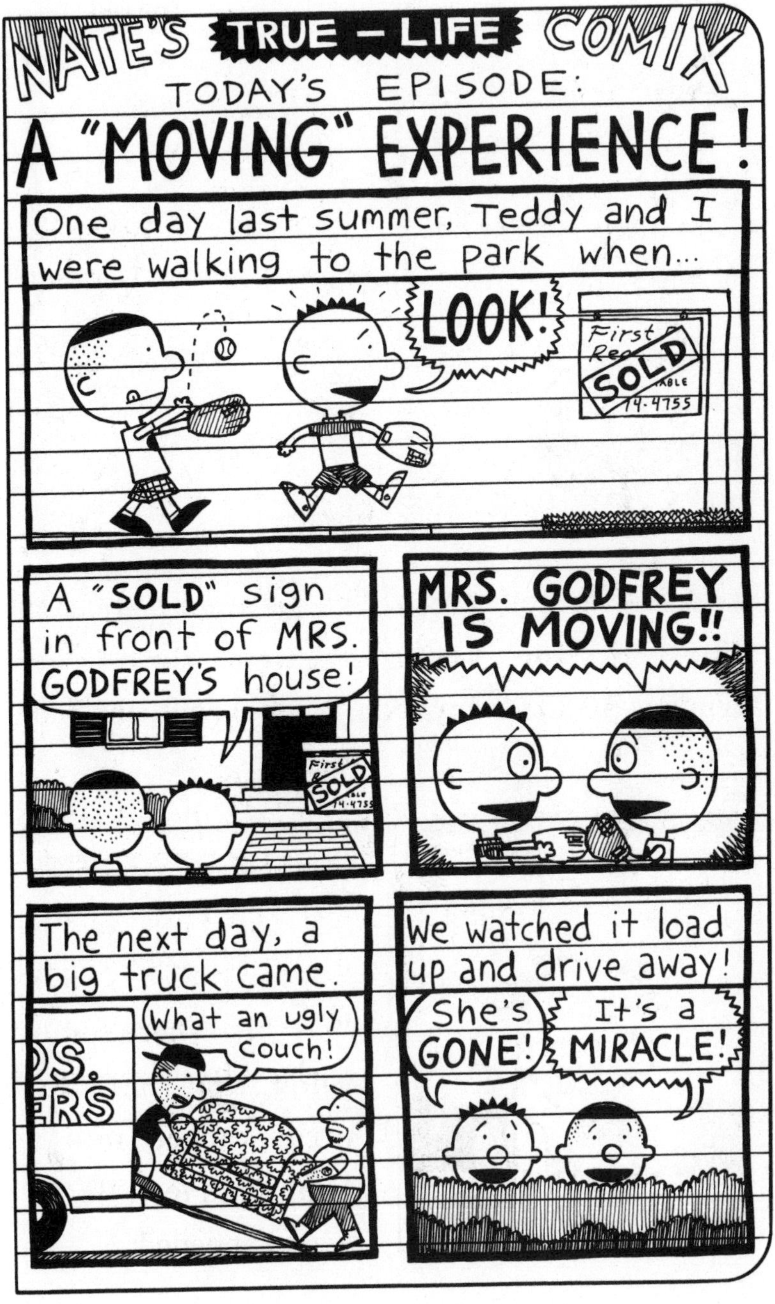
NATE'S TRUE-LIFE COMIX
TODAY'S EPISODE:
A "MOVING" EXPERIENCE!
One day last summer, Teddy and I were walking to the park when...
LOOK!
First
SOLD
74-4755
A "SOLD" sign in front of MRS. GODFREY'S house!
MRS. GODFREY IS MOVING!!
The next day, a big truck came.
What an ugly couch!
We watched it load up and drive away!
She's GONE!
It's a MIRACLE!

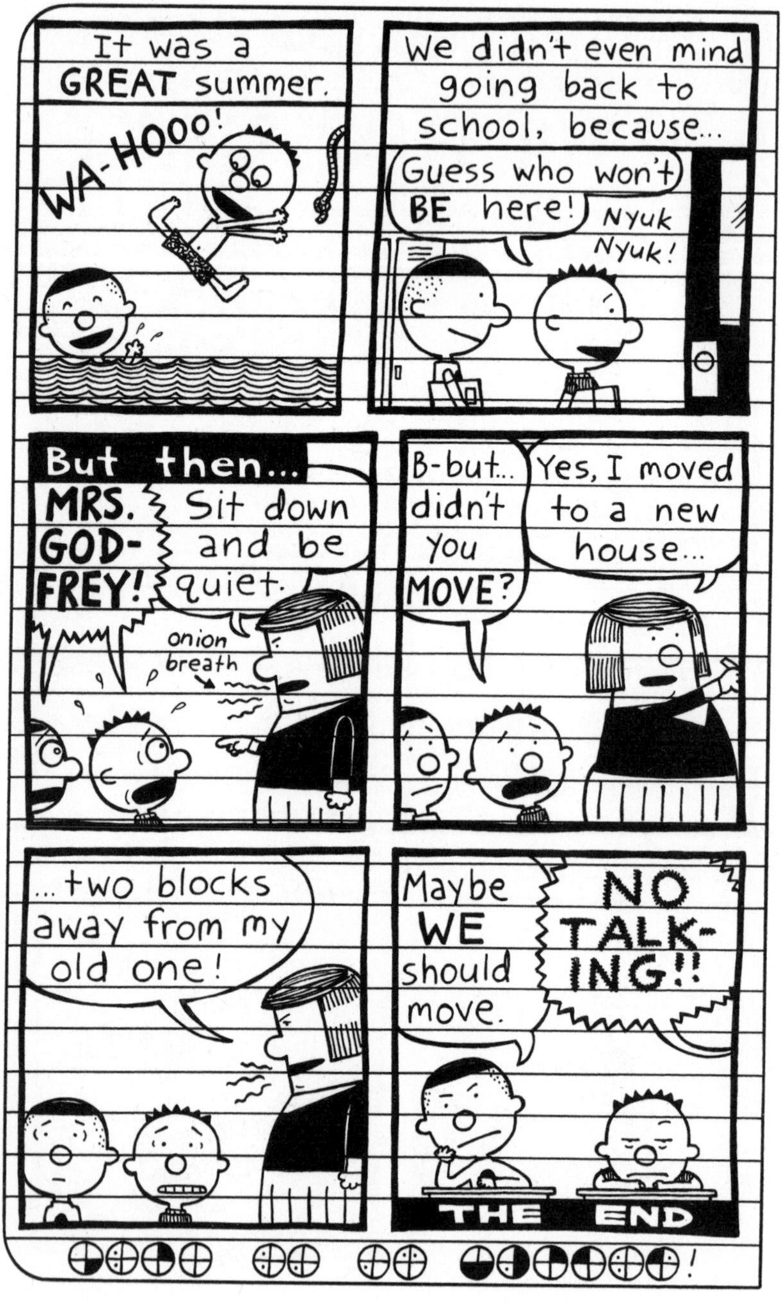

It was a GREAT summer.
WA-HOOO!
We didn't even mind going back to school, because...
Guess who won't BE here!
Nyuk Nyuk!
But then...
MRS. GOD-FREY!
Sit down and be quiet.
onion breath
B-but... didn't you MOVE?
Yes, I moved to a new house...
...two blocks away from my old one!
Maybe WE should move.
NO TALKING!!
THE END

My mood hasn't improved much by Monday morning, as the guys and I take the long, slow walk toward Jefferson.

We turn to see Dee Dee running after us. Of course. Who ELSE would scream "yoo-hoo" at 7:30 on a Monday morning?

"EXCITING?" I repeat in disbelief.

"Oh, sure," says Teddy, with a what-planet-are-you-from eye roll.

"I won't mind that one bit!" Dee Dee counters. "When people laugh, it means they NOTICE you!"

That shuts Dee Dee up . . . for maybe two seconds.
Then she drops THIS one on us:

We stop dead in our tracks. The three of us stare
at her, completely dumbstruck.

"Well, you ARE!" she says. "Why are you so afraid
of Jefferson?"

"We're not AFRAID of them," I shoot back.

"Nobody wins ALL the time," she declares.

I'LL BET **OUR** DRAMA CLUB COULD OUTPERFORM **THEIR** DRAMA CLUB!

Ooh. Thanks, Dee Dee. The next time some Jefferson goons are throwing snowballs at my head, I'll remind them that they're no match for P.S. 38 in the vitally important category of musical theater.

Meanwhile, she's still babbling. "All I'm saying is . . ."

EVERYONE CAN BE BEATEN!

EVERYONE HAS AN **ACHILLES'** HEEL!

Okay. Whatever THAT means. I don't really have time to think about it, because . . .

"So are we!" agrees Dee Dee, who's apparently elected herself our official spokesperson.

"There's still plenty of time before homeroom," Mrs. Williger tells us.

At HOME? Yeah, sure. This place is about as homey as the Grand Canyon.

Francis is right. The more we look around, the more there is to see.

"This is quite a place, isn't it, kids?"

"How come you're HERE?" Teddy asks him. "I thought you were fixing up OUR school."

He chuckles. "I'll leave that to people who know what they're doing . . . like Dee Dee's father."

"So the teachers from P.S. 38 are here at Jefferson, too?" Francis asks.

"Absolutely!" he answers.

Nuts. My chance for a two-week break from Mrs. Godfrey just got flushed.

Sure, bring it on, big fella. Considering how SWANKY this school is . . .

Principal Nichols leads us through a maze of hall-ways and down a flight of stairs.

"Almost there!" he says cheerfully, as he pushes open a metal door. But hold on . . . what's with the sign that says **EXIT** ?

"This is it!" Principal Nichols announces.

CHAPTER 7

We stand at the back door of Jefferson, staring out at . . . um . . . okay, I have no clue. What ARE those things?

"They're modular classrooms, Nate," Principal Nichols explains. "Jefferson used them last fall when they renovated their seventh grade wing . . ."

"Fortunately for us"?? Is he SERIOUS? What's fortunate about going to class in a giant SHOEBOX?

"Think of it as a grand adventure!" he tells us.

Uh . . . no, it won't. Not unless your camp's in the middle of a parking lot. But obviously, Principal Nichols HAS to say that. Making lousy stuff sound good is one of those things ALL grown-ups do.

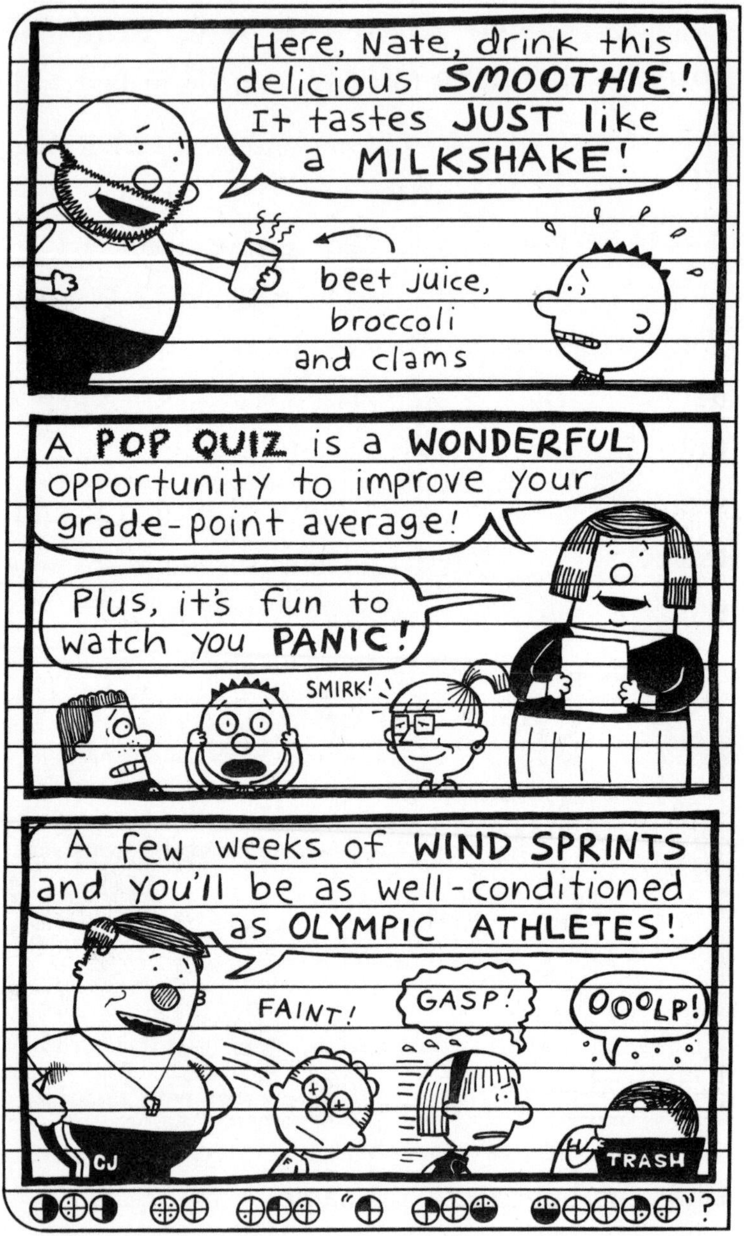
Here, Nate, drink this delicious SMOOTHIE! It tastes JUST like a MILKSHAKE!
beet juice, broccoli and clams
A POP QUIZ is a WONDERFUL opportunity to improve your grade-point average!
Plus, it's fun to watch you PANIC!
SMIRK!
A few weeks of WIND SPRINTS and you'll be as well-conditioned as OLYMPIC ATHLETES!
FAINT!
GASP!
OOOLP!
CJ
TRASH

Principal Nichols steers us toward one of the boxes. "You're in Room F."

"Hear that, Nate?" Teddy cracks. "Room F!"

We swing open the door, and there's Mrs. Godfrey. At P.S. 38, she's always surrounded by books, maps, and other torture devices. Here, all she's got is a flimsy little desk. It feels different.

Different, but exactly the same.

"Hmph," I grumble, looking around. "The REAL classrooms are all tricked out with murals and posters and stuff . . ."

Teddy nods. "Yeah, the only thing to look at is . . ." He points silently at Mrs. Godfrey.

"Not exactly a scenic view." I snicker.

"But look at the UPSIDE, guys," Francis chimes in. "Since they've separated us from the Jefferson students . . ."

Hm. That actually makes sense. As the classroom fills up and the bell rings, it starts to feel like just another brain-frying, butt-numbing school day. By the end of third period, we've almost forgotten we're even AT Jefferson.

And then comes lunch.

LUNCH FACT:
All-time worst dessert in P.S. 38 history:

STEWED PRUNES.

SPLUT!

Even a fancy-pants school like Jefferson has only one cafetorium. Which means they HAVE to share it with us. When the noon bell rings, we scurry away from our little boxcar village and into the main building.

"Excuse me, which way to the cafetorium?" Francis asks some Jefferson kid.

THAT WAY.

AND IT'S NOT A CAFETORIUM, IT'S A **FOOD COURT.**

"Oh, brother," Teddy mumbles as we continue down the hall. "Can this place get any more stuck-up?"

"Wonder what they call the BATHROOMS," Francis says.

We turn the corner and see a crowd of kids pouring into the cafeteria. (No, I will NOT call it the food court.) That's when it hits us: Something smells . . .

That's weird. We're not used to ANYTHING smelling good in school. Because, frankly, P.S. 38 is the stinkiest place on earth.

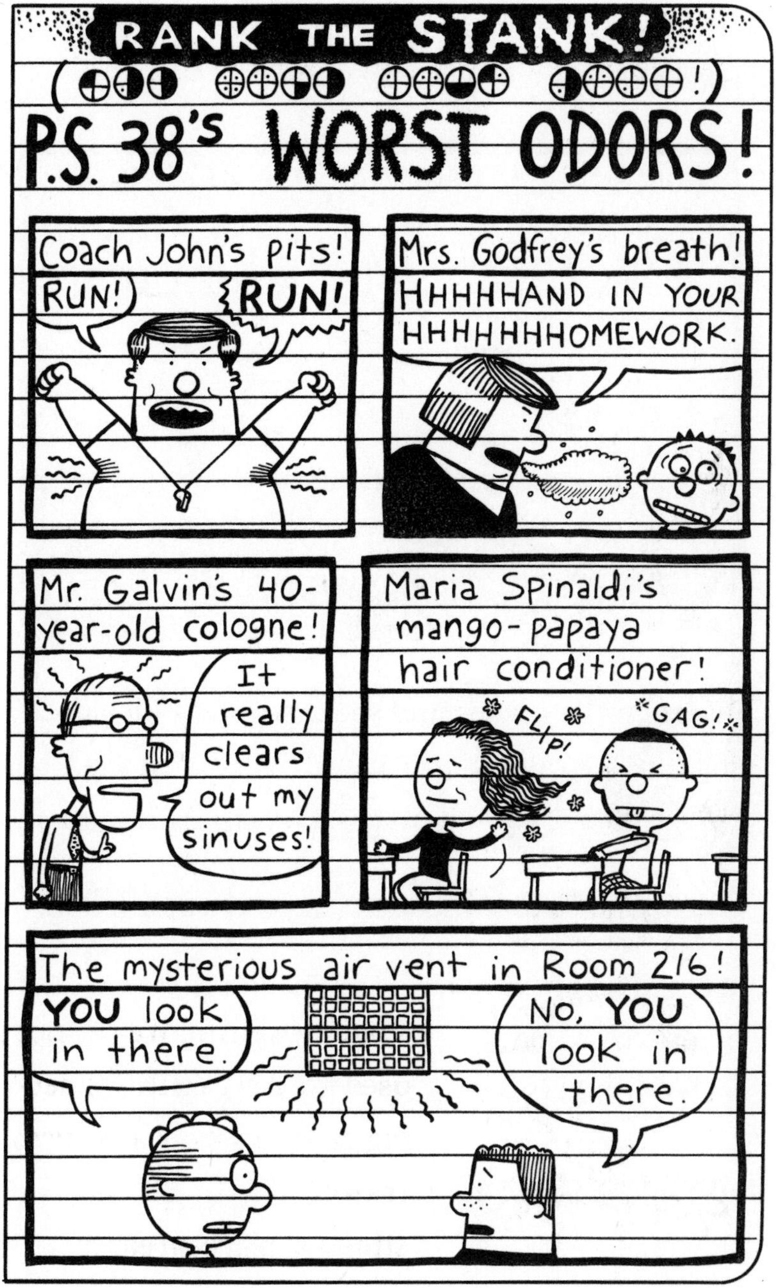
RANK THE STANK!
P.S. 38's WORST ODORS!
Coach John's pits!
RUN!
RUN!
Mrs. Godfrey's breath!
HHHHHAND IN YOUR HHHHHHHOMEWORK.
Mr. Galvin's 40-year-old cologne!
It really clears out my sinuses!
Maria Spinaldi's mango-papaya hair conditioner!
FLIP!
GAG!
The mysterious air vent in Room 216!
YOU look in there.
No, YOU look in there.

"Holy COW!" Teddy exclaims. "Can you believe this MENU?"

We can't believe our eyes. There's not a stewed prune in sight. Okay, we don't have to like Jefferson. But we can like their FOOD.

"What are we waiting for?" Francis says.

I spin around and spot Chad with his tailbone pillow . . . and look who's giving him the evil eye: Nolan. Teddy's right. This IS trouble.

"You're not at P.S. 38 anymore!" he sneers.

That's just wrong. Chad's the smallest kid in the sixth grade. AND he's hurt. The last thing he needs is a scuzzbucket like Nolan piling on.

"Or maybe it's NOT a toilet seat!" Nolan laughs.

I look for a teacher, but there aren't any. Typical. When you don't want them around, they're on you

like white on rice. But when you actually NEED
one? Good luck.

I feel my hands curl into fists. I'm no match for
Nolan. But SOMEBODY'S got to help Chad.

She marches over to Nolan and sticks her finger
right in his chest. "You give him back his pillow!"
she demands.

Nolan does a quick three sixty to make sure no teachers are watching. Then he slaps Dee Dee's hand away. "Beat it," he growls.

"Dee Dee's going to get herself killed," Francis says. I take a deep breath.

We park ourselves next to Dee Dee and Chad. "Come on, Nolan," Teddy says. "Knock it off."

He laughs right in Teddy's face. "Why?" he asks.

Hm. Okay, so much for Dad's bully theory.

Thanks for the wisdom, Dad. I'll file that away with all your other brilliant theories, like "Making your bed every day helps you live longer" and

"If you really get to know her, Mrs. Godfrey is probably a very nice person."

"Give it here!" Dee Dee says suddenly, trying to snatch the pillow from Nolan. But he's too quick for her.

He tosses it toward one of his crew, but it veers the tiniest bit off target.

By the time I realize I'm losing my balance, it's too late. There's no way to stop myself. Look out below.

Oof. I lie there stunned, hoping I didn't just join Chad in the bruised tailbone club.

"Good gravy! Nate, are you all right?" It's Principal Nichols. Great timing. NOW he shows up?

Mrs. Williger is here, too. But she doesn't look quite as friendly as she did this morning.

"Horseplay?" I protest. "But I wasn't . . ."

"We'll sort it out later, Nate," Principal Nichols tells me. "Let's get you up on your feet."

"What hurts?" he asks.

"My wrist!" I groan. I try to flex it, and the pain hits about a fifty on a scale of one to ten.

"Is he going to live?" asks Dee Dee.

"I think he'll make it," says Principal Nichols, lifting me off the floor.

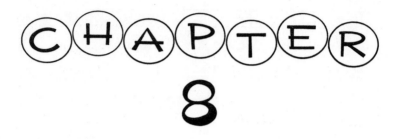

CHAPTER 8

"You know, that's not a bad joke," Teddy says as we file into the art room the next morning. "For a principal."

"Joke, shmoke," I grumble. "What's funny about a broken wrist?"

Oh, sure, Francis, it's a RIOT. And having a hunk of plaster wrapped around my hand for the next month should be a barrel of laughs.

I used to think it might be kind of COOL to have a cast. Last year, when Eric Fleury broke his arm, everyone treated him like Joe  Celebrity. All the girls were lining up for Eric time.

Suddenly the guy was a total babe magnet. (And, PS: All he did was fall down in the school yard while doing cheesy kung fu moves! At least I got hurt trying to help Chad.)

Anyway, Eric's moment of glory lasted about three minutes. After that, he said having a cast  turned into a major pain— and, boy, was he right. This thing is hot. It itches like crazy. And it's already starting to smell like Coach John's tube socks.

But you know the worst part about it? It's on my right hand. My DRAWING hand.

Brilliant deduction, Chad. There's only one little problem: I CAN'T DRAW!!

Oh, I've TRIED. It's the first thing I did when I got home from the hospital yesterday. But I can't even hold a pencil with this stupid cast on. It's like wearing a cement mitten.

So then I went with plan B: drawing left-handed.

Pathetic, right? I did better drawings back in KINDERGARTEN. And Dad made it worse by doing that fake praise thing parents always do. I hate that.

So now you know why I'm not exactly turning cartwheels when Mr. Rosa tells us to get to work. But I give it a shot.

"Maybe you should try sticking the pencil up your nose," Teddy cracks, after watching me draw a dog that looks more like a radioactive spider. ——————>

"Maybe YOU should," I snap back.

"I don't have a broken wrist," he reminds me.

"Okay, everyone, five-minute warning!" Mr. Rosa calls out. As we all start cleaning up, he stops by our table.

"Do you kids remember Mrs. Everett?" he asks.

"Sure!" says Francis. "She came to our Doodlers meeting!"

When science ends (and not a moment too soon, because Mr. Galvin was about to hit a new low on the Charisma meter), the Doodlers head for Mrs. Everett's room . . .

. . . along with our newest member.

THIS IS SO **EXCITING!** I'VE NEVER BEEN TO A CARTOONING CLUB MEETING! WHAT DO YOU THINK IT'LL BE LIKE? HOW MANY KIDS FROM JEFFERSON WILL BE THERE? I CAN'T WAIT TO SEE EVERYONE'S COMICS! HAVE YOU EVER MET ANY FAMOUS CARTOONISTS? WHAT IF **I** BECOME A FAMOUS CARTOONIST SOMEDAY?

Dee Dee's yapping like a Chihuahua on a sugar buzz. I guess she's all amped up about listening to the almighty C.I.C. tell us how TALENTED they are. Or maybe she can't wait to see one of my amazingly lame left-handed drawings.

"It seems pretty quiet," Teddy says as we approach an open doorway. "Are you sure we're in the right place?"

"You're ABSOLUTELY in the right place!" says Mrs. Everett, waving us into the room.

Here's a shocker: Jefferson has the swankiest art studio I've ever seen. And it's packed with kids drawing comics.

A few look up and nod, but most of them don't even notice us. They just keep drawing. Wow, it's like an ASSEMBLY LINE in here.

"Yes." Mrs. Everett nods. "They have a deadline."

"It's a local literary magazine," Mrs. Everett explains. "It's sponsoring a kids' writing contest!"

Chad looks baffled. "But . . . comics aren't WRITING!"

"SURE they are!" she says.

"I have entry forms, if you're interested," she adds.

"I'll be right back." Mrs. Everett smiles.

Everybody chatters excitedly as she goes to her desk. Except me. I don't say a word.

"What's wrong with this picture?" Teddy asks.

"Huh?" I mumble.

"Because I can't enter the CONTEST, Einstein,"
I answer. "I'm halfway through my most hilarious
'Doctor Cesspool' adventure EVER . . . "

Mrs. Everett is back. "Why not collaborate?" she
suggests. "You could write the rest of the story,
and couldn't one of your fellow Doodlers supply
the artwork?"

What? Whoa, WHOA. No offense, Dee Dee, but you're not exactly at the top of my A-list. I'll team up with Francis or Teddy or . . .

"I think that's a GREAT idea!" Mr. Rosa just appeared out of nowhere at our table.

Oh, come on. I already took her to the dance and carried her home on my back. Haven't I suffered enough? But Mr. Rosa's wearing his happy adviser face. Nuts. I guess it's settled.

"Just hand them back by Friday, along with your comics!"

Dee Dee scoots her chair over next to mine. "Tell me about Doctor Cesspool! What's his story?"

"Yeah, but this isn't the Drama Club!" I hiss at her. "It's . . . it's . . ." My voice trails off.

"What's the matter?" she whispers.

I look around the room at all the Jefferson kids bent over their drawings.

I'm not used to this. Doodlers meetings are FUN. Mr. Rosa lets us talk and play the radio and eat snacks. This is different.

"You're right, Nate, it IS awfully quiet," Mr. Rosa says. Then he gives me a wink. "But maybe the Doodlers can find a way to liven things up!"

He walks over to Mrs. Everett. "May we show you and your students a fun drawing game?"

"Of course!" she answers.

"Grab a fresh sheet of paper, everyone!" Mr. Rosa announces.

"You'll figure it out as we go along!" Mr. Rosa tells them. "At the end of the game, you'll have drawn a complete character from head to toe!"

"Except the characters might not HAVE heads!" Chad laughs. "OR toes!"

"I'll go first!" I say. "Draw . . . ummmm . . ."

". . . and that's ALL you draw!" Mr. Rosa says. "Until the NEXT person tells us what to add on! How 'bout it, Teddy?"

"Ah!" Mr. Rosa exclaims. "So now it's up to YOU, cartoonists, to decide exactly WHERE to draw that peg leg!"

One Jefferson kid looks confused. "My drawing is just a nose and a peg leg, floating in space."

"Perfect! You're doing it right!" says Mr. Rosa. "Who's next?"

Like I always say: There's nothing like a game of Add-On to break the ice. When the time comes for everyone to show off their drawings, we're all cracking up. Every single drawing is completely hilarious. And believe it or not, guess whose is my favorite?

"That was FABULOUS!" Dee Dee says as we leave Mrs. Everett's room an hour later. "I should have joined the Doodlers YEARS ago!"

"We didn't EXIST years ago," Francis points out.

"It was a good meeting," I say, "once those C.I.C. kids actually started TALKING to us."

"Yeah, some of them were pretty nice!" Dee Dee agrees. "SEE, you guys . . . ?"

JEFFERSON ISN'T SO BAD **AFTER** ALL!

CHAPTER 9

CAVALIER PRIDE
AHEM! UM... HI!
!

Wowza! A girl is walking . . .

No, wait. Let me start again.

A TURBO CUTE girl is walking this way, and . . .

. . . she's looking right at ME! JACKPOT!!

"You're Nate, right?" she asks.

"Very smooth," Teddy mutters. I give him a quick kick in the shin.

"I just want to tell you," the mystery girl says, "everyone thought it was GREAT the way you stood up to Nolan in the food court yesterday!"

So THIS is what it was like for Eric Fleury. "Sure!"
I say. "I think I've got a pen here somewhere . . ."

"Oh, I've got one," she says quickly, pulling out a
marker the size of a salami.

Wait, what? She disappears around the corner, and
I hear an explosion of laughter. A vise tightens in
my stomach as I look down at my wrist.

Then she's back. Only this time, she's not alone.

Away they go, laughing their heads off. Bet you a buck they're not discussing knock-knock jokes.

"That was tricky dirt," Artur says.

"You mean 'dirty trick,'" says Francis.

Dee Dee throws up her hands. "Don't blame ME!" she protests. "I was just trying to look on the BRIGHT side!"

"There IS no bright side." Chad sighs.

What ABOUT it? I'll be watching from the bench. I can't play basketball with this giant plaster sweatband on my wrist.

"Wait, won't the game be postponed?" Francis asks. "The gym at P.S. 38 is in no condition to—"

Teddy cuts him off. "We're not playing at P.S. 38. They're moving the game HERE. To Jefferson."

NOW what? Is this another example of Dee Dee's terminal case of Look-at-Me-itis, or . . .

"No," she says, hands on her hips. "I'm simply pointing out how useless it is to stand around complaining . . ."

Apparently, while I wasn't paying attention, Dee Dee became a basketball expert. "Okay, then, Coach," I say sarcastically. "How DO we win?"

"By finding Jefferson's weakness, of course."

FINDING THEIR **WEAKNESS**!!! **JEEPERS**, WHY DIDN'T **I** THINK OF THAT? IT'S SO **SIMPLE**!!

"I never said it was simple," she tells me. "But Jefferson's not indestructible."

? ?

THEY'VE **GOT** TO HAVE AN **ACHILLES' HEEL**!

That's the SECOND time she's said that. Who's this Achilles dude? And what does his HEEL have to do with anything?

Later, at home, I decide to find out.

"Dad," I ask, "what's an Achilles' heel?"

Who asked YOU, Ellen? But before I can stop her, she's shoving some papers in my face. "I wrote this report in fourth grade!" she brags.

Difference number 7,387,289 between me and Ellen: The reports I did in fourth grade are buried in a landfill somewhere. The ones SHE did are carefully stored in a file cabinet in her room, right next to her priceless collection of plastic panda figurines.

The Myth Of
ACHILLES A+☺

by Ellen Wright   Grade 4

In ancient Greece, the goddess **Thetis** fell in love with a mortal named **Peleus**. They had a son and named him **Achilles**.

When Achilles was a baby, Thetis decided that she wanted Achilles to be immortal like she was, so she carried him to the **River Styx**. Everything that touched the river's magical waters became **indestructible**. Thetis held Achilles by the heel and dipped him in the river, not realizing that his **HEEL** never touched the water!!!

Achilles grew up and became the greatest warrior in the land. The **Trojan War** was being fought between Greece and Troy. Achilles was on the side of the

(turn page!!)——→

Greeks. At first, Achilles re-
fused to fight because he was
mad at **Agamemnon**, the leader
of the Greek army. But after
his best friend **Patroclus** was
killed, Achilles joined the battle.
  Thousands and thousands of
Trojan arrows struck Achilles, but
they had no effect. THEN...

One arrow hit him in the **HEEL**-
the only part of his body left
untouched by the protective waters
of the River Styx!! Because of
that, Achilles died.
  So when people say something is
your **"Achilles' heel,"** they mean it's
a tiny weakness that might cause
you big trouble. I think that's
interesting!! Don't **YOU**????
The End

Huh. Yeah, that IS pretty interesting. But why should I tell HER that? It's not my job to inflate Ellen's ego. She's got her own built-in pump.

There's the doorbell. I'll get it.

Until this very second, I thought Dee Dee was a little unusual. Okay, maybe more than a little . . . but basically harmless. Now I'm not so sure.

She might have some deeper issues.

"Why are you dressed like a cat?" I ask her. I COULD have said: "Have you completely lost your mind?"

"I'm doing a dress rehearsal!" she answers happily. "And I'm not just ANY cat! . . ."

"I'm going to wear this to the game Saturday and cheer us on to victory! I'll be our mascot!"

"Are you CRAZY?" I shout. "You can't show up at Jefferson looking like THAT!"

"Well, of COURSE not, silly!" she says.

"But bobcats are FIERCE!" I tell her. "You look like you should be rolling around on the floor with a ball of YARN!"

"Oh, pshaw," she says.

"If I'm going to finish your 'Doctor Cesspool' story in time to enter the contest, I'd better get started!"

Oh, right, I forgot about that.

DEE DEE'S IMITATION OF A GIANT **FUR BALL** GAVE ME A **BRAIN CRAMP**!

I grab a bunch of paper from my room. But I don't like this. What if Dee Dee totally messes up my comic? What if she makes it all . . . well . . . DEE DEE-ish?

THE FIRST PART'S ALL DONE... AND THE SECOND PART I SKETCHED LIGHTLY IN PENCIL. SO ALL YOU HAVE TO DO IS FINISH IT IN PEN. YOU DON'T HAVE TO... UH... ADD ANY WEIRD DETAILS, OR... I MEAN... JUST DON'T DO ANY... ANYTHING... UM... Y'KNOW... ANY CHANGES OR... UH... WHAT I MEAN IS...

"Nate, RELAX!" she says. "I'm not going to ruin your comic!"

So what happens? Two days later, Dee Dee submits "Doctor Cesspool" WITHOUT EVEN SHOWING ME THE FINISHED COMIC!

"I didn't have TIME to show it to you!" she explains at the end of school on Friday.

It's not that I don't believe her. It's just that I wanted to SEE it first. After all, "Doctor Cesspool" is MY creation.

But what's done is done. I can't do anyth—

"In here!" whispers a voice.

"Chad?" Dee Dee says. "Is that you?"

"Yeah!" he whispers back. "Come on in! . . ."

Dee Dee and I squeeze inside.

"Close the door, you guys," says Chad. "I don't think we're supposed to be in here."

It's basically a king-size closet, packed with all sorts of stuff: old science equipment that looks like its last stop was Frankenstein's lab, a couple of antique bicycles, a lawn mower, a stuffed owl . . .

"Ooh!" Dee Dee says . . .

"ANOTHER one?" I say. "They've already got one on display in the front hall!"

"Yeah," Chad says. "Why do they need TWO?"

"Because they're twice as good as everyone else," I grumble. "They're JEFFERSON."

"Hiding," he answers.

"Hiding?" I ask as I pop back into the hallway.

"THERE you are, Tiny!" Nolan sneers at Chad.

"We weren't playing any games," I say through gritted teeth.

"Oh, that's right, I FORGOT!" Nolan crows. "P.S. 38 STINKS at games!"

"The only thing you'll find out is that a BOBCAT is no match for a CAVALIER!" Nolan says.

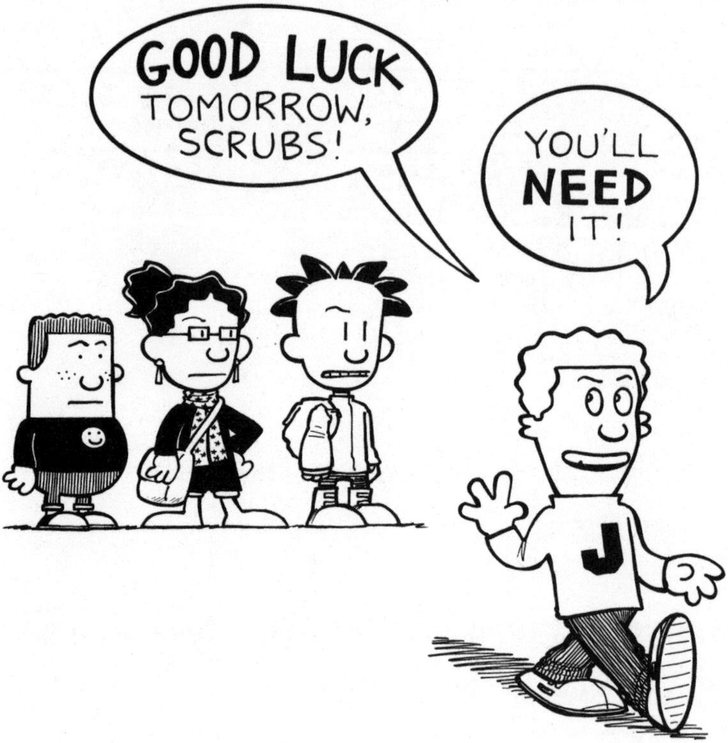
GOOD LUCK TOMORROW, SCRUBS!
YOU'LL NEED IT!

CHAPTER
10

You can't always believe everything you see. Like this scoreboard, for instance.

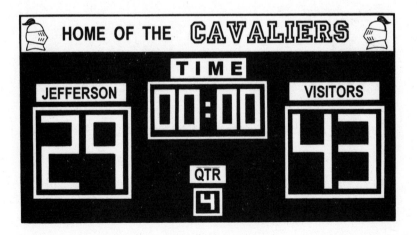

You're probably thinking: Wow! P.S. 38 did it!
They beat Jefferson, 43–29!

Uh, wrong.

See, the scoreboard only has room for TWO-DIGIT
numbers. We scored 43, all right. But Jefferson
didn't score 29. They scored . . .

And all I could do was sit there and WATCH it.
I felt like running onto the court and clubbing
somebody over the head with my cast . . . but I
stopped myself. I didn't want to rebreak my wrist.

Chad was on the bench beside me, taking pictures for the yearbook. Great. We can stick these on a page called "most humiliating moments."

Poor Coach. He's usually Peter Positive, but he looked like he'd just lost (a) his dog, (b) his best friend, and (c) a basketball game . . . BY EIGHTY-SIX POINTS!!

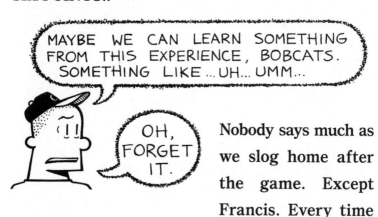

Nobody says much as we slog home after the game. Except Francis. Every time we lose to Jefferson, he has to analyze exactly what went wrong.

"Offense, defense, rebounding . . ." he says. "They beat us in every part of the game."

"But they didn't HAVE a mascot," Chad says.

"Exactly!" answers Dee Dee. "So I won!"

"That's ridiculous," Francis says.

"Guys!" I shout. "Let's DO it!"

"Do what?" everyone asks.

"Right!" I say. "They've spanked us at all the OFFICIAL activities . . ."

...SO LET'S TRY AN **UN**OFFICIAL ONE!

Francis is skeptical. "Like what?" he asks.

"Leave that to ME!" I tell him.

I'LL GIVE IT THE **GREAT BRAIN** TREATMENT!

Have you ever read the Great Brain books? They're awesome. The main character, Tom, is a genius. Like me. And whenever he has a problem that needs solving, he thinks about it right before he goes to bed. Then his Great Brain comes up with a perfect solution while he sleeps. When he wakes up in the morning, he's got an answer.

Except it doesn't work. When I open my eyes at 8:00 a.m. . . .

. . . all I can remember is that I was having a dream about Mrs. Godfrey drowning in an ocean of Cheez Doodles. But no great ideas. No perfect solutions. I guess my brain took the night off.

And the morning, too. The hours roll by, and I'm still stumped. I haven't felt this clueless since that last science test. (Who CARES about the digestive system of a fruit fly?) Anyway, I need help.

And I know just who to ask. Someone with experience. Someone who knows what he's talking about.

Mr. Rosa will understand. After all, he's been teaching at P.S. 38 since before I was BORN.

I cut right to the chase. "We want to challenge Jefferson to . . . um . . . something."

"Hm," he says. "What kind of something?"

"That's what I can't figure out," I admit.

"Well, nobody's good at EVERYTHING," he says. "And don't sell P.S. 38 short. Remember, YOU have strengths, TOO."

"Think of that C.I.C. meeting we went to the other day," he explains. "Didn't you think it was kind of BORING?"

"Oh yeah, it was a no-fun zone in there," I agree, "until we showed them how to play Add-On."

"Right. By the way, who taught YOU that game?"

Mr. Rosa smiles. "I see," he says. "Very creative."

Then he pulls two booklets out of a drawer and lays them on the table. "You might recognize one of these," he tells me.

"It sure is," he says. "And the other is a collection of drawings by the Jefferson C.I.C. Take a look."

I get that familiar queasy feeling in my stomach as I flip through the booklet.

"They can really draw," is all I can say.

"Oh, yes, they're very good," Mr. Rosa agrees.

"Huh? There are no STORIES in here," I say, scanning the booklet again. "Just drawings."

"Right," he says. "But YOUR booklet is FULL of stories. Some very FUNNY stories, by the way!"

"I repeat," Mr. Rosa says, his eyes twinkling. "Very creative."

"Yeah, but . . . I still don't know what kind of competition to have with Jefferson!" I say as Mr. Rosa shows me to the door.

"You'll think of something," he says simply.

Strengths. Okay, I get the message: I'm creative. But how's that going to help us beat Jefferson in any kind of showdown?

THAT'S IT! Maybe I didn't find an answer in my sleep like the Great Brain, but I figured something out eventually. It just goes to show . . .

I slam into Dee Dee, who for some reason is standing right in the middle of the sidewalk. "Oh, my LEG!" she moans as she gets to her feet. "I think I FRACTURED my KNEECAP!"

"Save the drama for your mama, Dee Dee," I say, "and listen to this great idea!"

Her face lights up as I describe my plan, and pretty soon she's hopping around like Spitsy with a kibble buzz. So much for that fractured kneecap.

When we get to Dee Dee's, she pulls out some poster board and markers and gets to work. I call the guys to fill them in. We all agree: This is our best chance ever to finally beat Jefferson.

First thing Monday morning, we do a little decorating in the Jefferson lobby.

"You're challenging us to a snow sculpture contest?" Nolan sneers.

"Surprise," Teddy whispers in my ear.

"We're not planning on losing," Dee Dee answers.

One of Nolan's groupies shoots us a suspicious look. "How do we decide who wins?"

"One judge from each school. That's fair," Francis says.

Nolan shrugs. "Whatever. It's not going to matter WHO the judges are . . ."

They walk off, leaving us standing in the ginormous lobby full of trophies, plaques, and championship banners.

Chad looks worried. "They seem pretty confident."

"Yeah," I say. "But not as confident as I am."

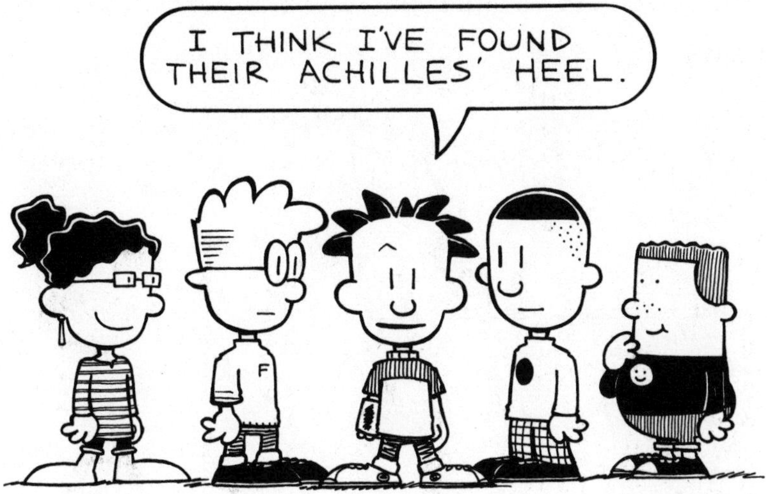
I THINK I'VE FOUND THEIR ACHILLES' HEEL.

CHAPTER
11

The school is buzzing all week until—FINALLY!—
Saturday's here. The air's cold but not TOO cold.
The snow's wet but not TOO wet. It's perfect sculp-
ture weather.

All of us swing into action. By "us," I mean us KIDS. The Ultimate Snowdown is for kids only. We don't want a bunch of grown-ups trying to hog the glory. You know what happens when so-called adults try to take over. ➤

TRAUMATIC FLASHBACK: Dad "helps" me build my car for the Timber Scout Driftwood Derby.

Besides, it's not like we need any more people. We've got tons of kids ready to roll, and so does Jefferson. At least I THINK they do. It's hard to tell, because . . .

"What's THAT all about?" Teddy asks.

"Maybe they think we'll try to copy their sculpture," Francis says.

Nolan and another kid sneak out from behind the school, pulling a sled loaded up with . . . well, whatever it is, it's all covered in blankets. We watch as they disappear behind the tarp.

"I wonder what that was," Chad says.

"Maybe it was a dead body," Dee Dee whispers.

"If we stand around yakking about what JEFFERSON's doing, we'll never finish OUR sculpture!" Francis says.

Reality check: We've only got six hours. If we want to create a masterpiece by 3:00 this afternoon . . .

So we do. Once we stop worrying about that giant tarp, we start humming along like a well-oiled machine. Some kids toss snow on the pile, others pack it down, and those of us with actual

artistic talent do the rest. Our sculpture starts to take shape. And (I'm not just saying this because it was my idea) it looks AWESOME.

I think it'll be good enough . . . if my theory about Jefferson's weak spot is right. But we're not going to find out for sure until . . .

"Let's start with Jefferson's entry," Mr. Rosa says.

A couple of kids from the C.I.C. start to lower the tarp. I hold my breath. This is it: almighty Jefferson's moment of truth.

The cheers from Jefferson almost blow my ears off. Our side looks stunned. There's no doubt: It's a pretty amazing sculpture.

But I'm not looking at the cavalier. I'm looking at Mr. Rosa and Mrs. Everett. And you know what?

The two of them inspect the sculpture from every angle. Then they put their heads together, talking in whispers. Finally . . .

"There's a real suit of armor under here," Mr. Rosa says.

It gets deadly quiet. I sneak a peek at Nolan. He looks . . . NERVOUS.

"That explains the impressive degree of realism," Mrs. Everett says. She turns to Nolan. "Did you use the old suit of armor from the storage room?"

She nods. "That's true. Technically, no rules were broken. But just covering something with snow instead of sculpting it yourselves . . ."

"I KNEW it!" I whisper.

Chad looks puzzled. "You knew they were going to swipe that suit of armor?"

I shake my head. "No, but I knew they're not as CREATIVE as we are!"

We wade through the snow toward our sculpture. Mr. Rosa taps me on the shoulder. "Nate, tell us about P.S. 38's entry."

"Sure!" I answer. "It's called . . ."

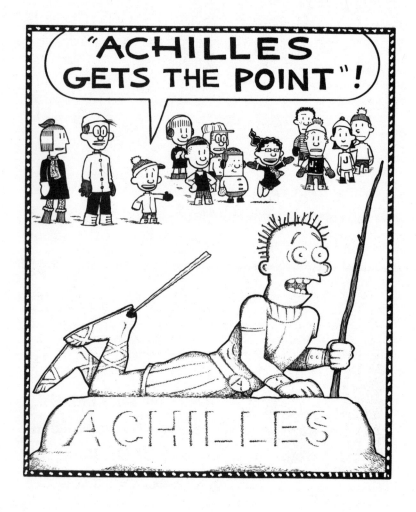

"What a dynamic pose!" Mrs. Everett exclaims. "And I love the expression on his face!"

"How did you make the arrow?" Mr. Rosa asks, glancing at the Jefferson kids. "Did you pack snow around a REAL arrow?"

Mrs. Everett studies the blotch of red on Achilles' heel. "This isn't actual blood, I hope?"

"Well, you SUCCEEDED!" Mrs. Everett laughs. Then she nods at Mr. Rosa. He nods back. Here it comes.

"The judges are in agreement!" she announces.

"The winners of the Ultimate Snowdown ARE . . ."

...THE P.S. 38 BOBCATS!

We explode. Everyone goes crazy. I mean, CRAZY. Teddy's throwing handfuls of snow, Chad's doing snow angels, and Dee Dee's hugging anything that moves. Me? I just keep pinching myself. We finally did it. WE BEAT JEFFERSON!!!

Mrs. Everett finds me in the crowd. "Nate, congratulations! You and your classmates did a wonderful job!"

"Thanks," I say, ducking out of the way of a bear hug from Dee Dee.

"I'm curious, though," she says. "Why did you choose Achilles as a subject?"

"We just think it's a good story," I tell her. "Achilles thought he was indestructible. But the truth is . . ."

CHAPTER 12

P.S. 38 finally reopened on Monday. I never thought I'd say this, but . . .

"Nate and Dee Dee, you won third prize in the 'Story Spinners' kids' writing competition!"

"That means we beat Jefferson AGAIN!" I crow.

"Yes," Mr. Rosa says with a smile. "You've got a winning streak going!"

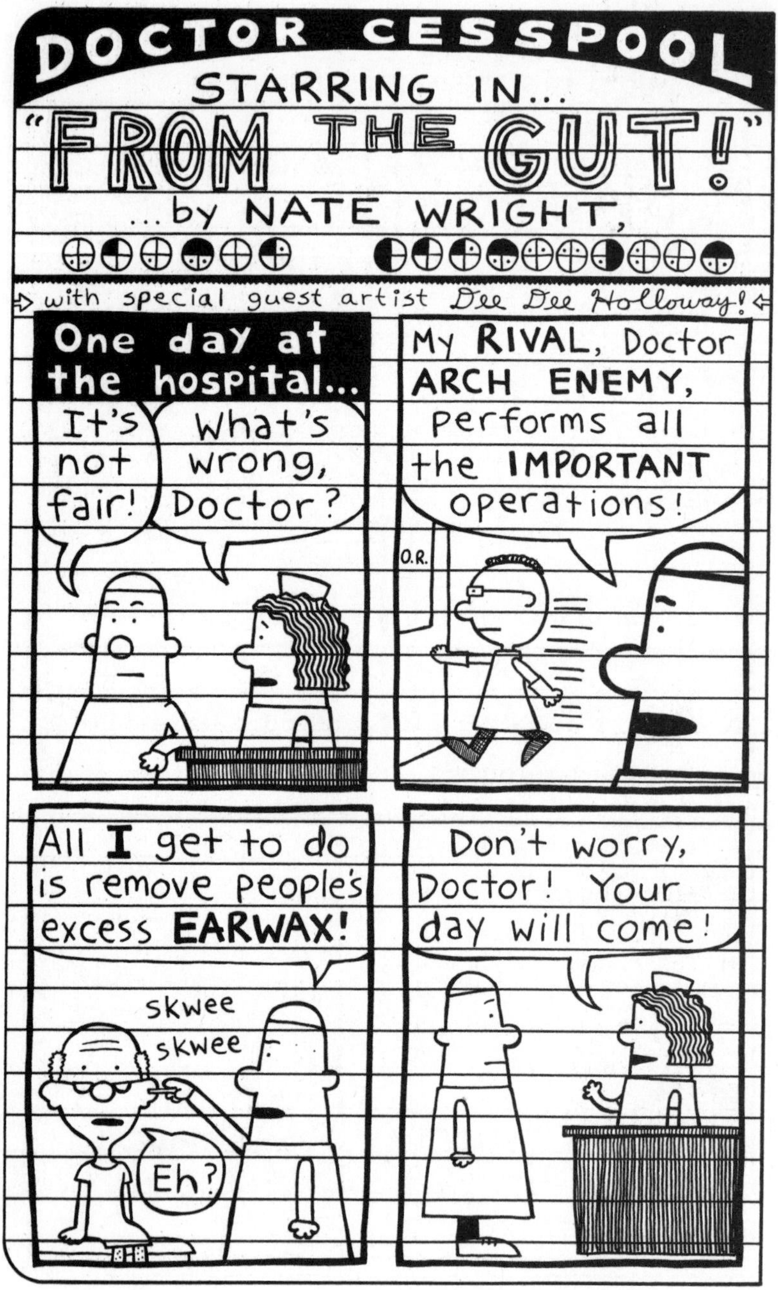
DOCTOR CESSPOOL
STARRING IN...
"FROM THE GUT!"
...by NATE WRIGHT,
with special guest artist Dee Dee Holloway!
One day at the hospital...
It's not fair!
What's wrong, Doctor?
My RIVAL, Doctor ARCH ENEMY, performs all the IMPORTANT operations!
O.R.
All I get to do is remove people's excess EARWAX!
skwee skwee
Eh?
Don't worry, Doctor! Your day will come!

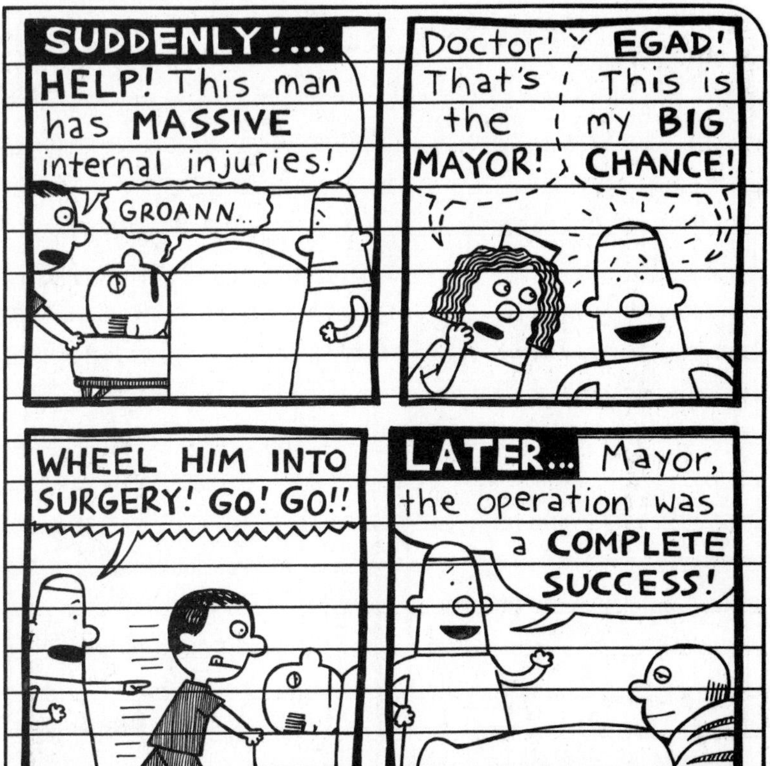

SUDDENLY!...
HELP! This man has MASSIVE internal injuries!
GROANN...
Doctor! That's the MAYOR!
EGAD! This is my BIG CHANCE!
WHEEL HIM INTO SURGERY! GO! GO!!
LATER... Mayor, the operation was a COMPLETE SUCCESS!
Attention!! Dee Dee's drawings start NOW!
I'm here! I'LL operate on the mayor!!
You're TOO LATE, Dr. Enemy!
I'VE already saved the Mayor's life!

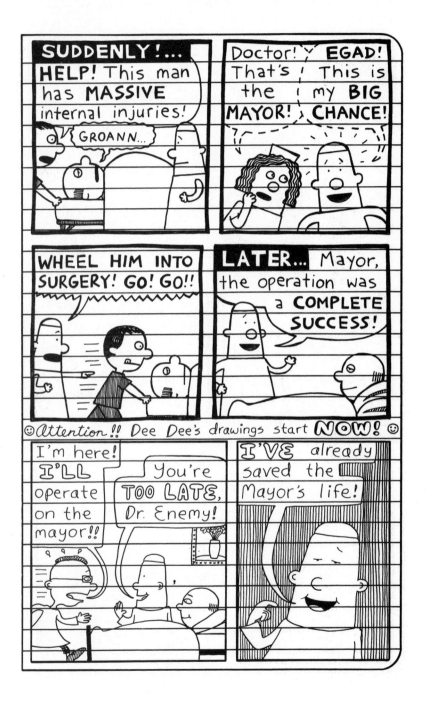

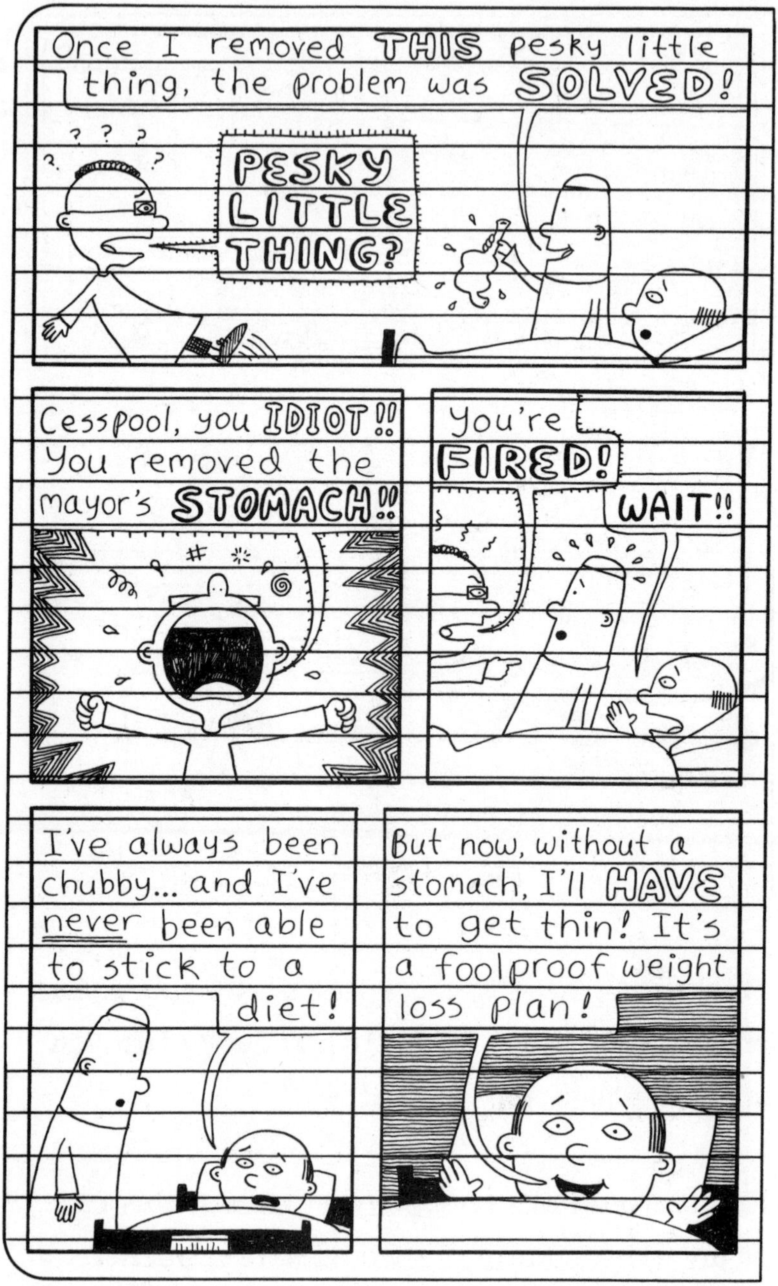
Once I removed THIS pesky little thing, the problem was SOLVED!
? ? ? ? ?
PESKY LITTLE THING?
Cesspool, you IDIOT!! You removed the mayor's STOMACH!!
You're FIRED!
WAIT!!
I've always been chubby... and I've never been able to stick to a diet!
But now, without a stomach, I'll HAVE to get thin! It's a foolproof weight loss plan!

"Wow!" I exclaim. "It turned out . . . GREAT!"

"Yeah, it's UNIQUE! I bet that's why you got a prize!" Francis says. "If you hadn't teamed up, you might not have won ANYTHING!"

Hm. Maybe that's true. Maybe without this cast on my wrist, none of this would have happened.

And it all started with my swan dive off that table in the Jefferson food court. Pretty funny, right? It was a total accident.

Lincoln Peirce

(pronounced "purse") is a cartoonist/writer and *New York Times* bestselling author of the hilarious Big Nate book series (www.bignatebooks.com), now published in twenty-seven countries worldwide and available as ebooks and audiobooks and as an app, Big Nate: Comix by U! He is also the creator of the comic strip *Big Nate*. It appears in over four hundred U.S. newspapers and online daily at www.gocomics.com/bignate. Lincoln's boyhood idol was Charles Schulz of *Peanuts* fame, but his main inspiration for Big Nate has always been his own experience as a sixth grader. Just like Nate, Lincoln loves comics, ice hockey, and Cheez Doodles (and dislikes cats, figure skating, and egg salad). His Big Nate books have been featured on *Today* and *Good Morning America* and in the *Boston Globe*, the *Los Angeles Times*, *USA Today*, and the *Washington Post*. He has also written for Cartoon Network and Nickelodeon. Lincoln lives with his wife and two children in Portland, Maine.

Also available as an ebook.

NATE ≠ NEAT

Have you ever scrambled the letters in your name to see if they spell anything else? Well, **I** have. And guess what: MY letters spell **N·E·A·T!**

Pretty ironic, right? Hey, I realize I'm not exactly Joe Tidy. **EVERYBODY** knows it. But that doesn't stop Francis, who color-codes his underwear, from pointing it out about a jillion times a day.

Your desk is **DISGUSTING.** You have paint on your shirt. Oh, and you have Cheez Doodle stains all over your face. What a SLOB you are!

Francis has been telling me to [shape] up my act since I poured [s]auce down his pants back [in ki]ndergarten. Of course, I've always ignored him. But then last week my sloppiness got Francis in trouble... and he **NEVER** gets in trouble!

I felt so bad about it, I decided to actually try to get neater. And thanks to

Teddy and his Uncle Pedro, the hypnotist, it's working... **TOO** well. All of the sudden, I'm starting to act **JUST LIKE FRANCIS!** Frankly, I think I'm losing my mind.

What a **MESS!** Read all about it in **BIG NATE FLIPS OUT!!**

BOB THE BOBCAT STARRING IN...

SNOWY, SNOWY KNIGHT

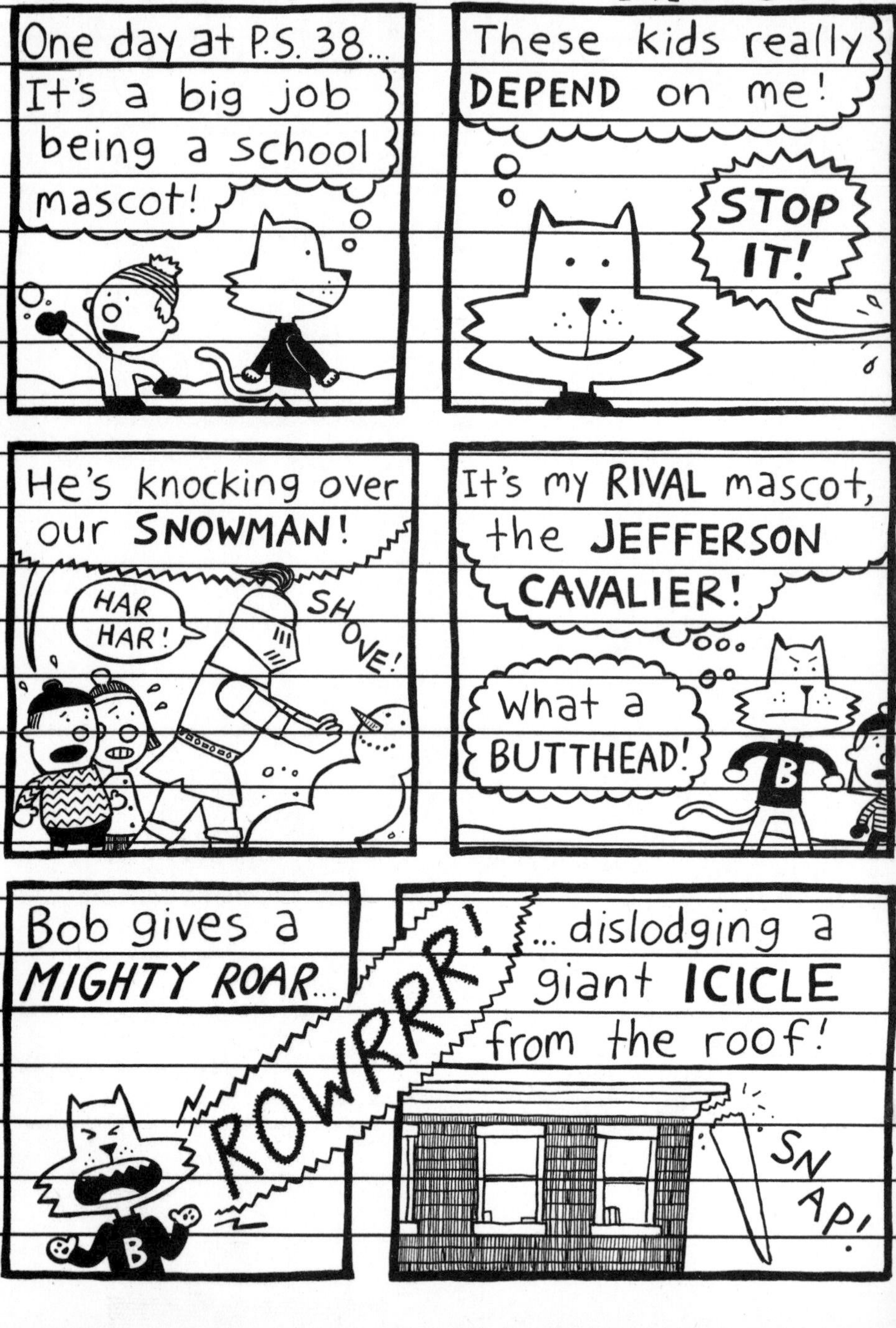

One day at P.S. 38...
It's a big job being a school mascot!
These kids really DEPEND on me!
STOP IT!
He's knocking over our SNOWMAN!
HAR HAR!
SHOVE!
It's my RIVAL mascot, the JEFFERSON CAVALIER!
What a BUTTHEAD!
B
Bob gives a MIGHTY ROAR...
ROWRRR!
B
...dislodging a giant ICICLE from the roof!
SNAP!